"No!"

Victoria grabbed his arm with both hands. "No. You can't. Please. I'll do anything." Tears filled her eyes. "I beg you. Don't lock him away. Take me instead. He offered me in the game. Did you tell him no, or did you accept? Was I in play? Did you win me?"

Kateb narrowed his gaze. "I knew he didn't mean it."

"You've spoken with him. You know he did. You took the bet. You played the hand. You won me. So take me instead."

"As what?"

"As whatever you want."

Dear Reader,

There is something spectacularly sexy about a dark, dangerous man on a horse that sets my heart beating faster and gives me that little tingle inside. My sheik books have allowed me to explore wonderful lands where there are castles and power and unbelievable wealth. They are safe havens, far from reality. Which is why I love them so.

This time around, I'm trying something a tiny bit different. *The Sheik and the Bought Bride* has an exciting premise: the heroine is won by the hero in a game of cards. Kateb believes Victoria is looking to marry into money, at any price. He vows to punish her in the name of all men who have been deceived by beautiful, scheming women.

There are a couple of flaws in his plan. First of all, Victoria isn't the villain he assumes. She's funny and brave and determined and unlike anyone he's ever met before. Second, he's not as immune to Victoria as he might think. What starts out as an attempt to punish quickly turns into something else. Something that very well might be love.

It is night in the desert. Quiet and still…until…

Best,

Susan Mallery

THE SHEIK AND THE BOUGHT BRIDE

SUSAN MALLERY

Silhouette

SPECIAL EDITION®

Published by Silhouette Books

America's Publisher of Contemporary Romance

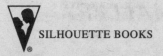

SILHOUETTE BOOKS

ISBN-13: 978-0-373-65481-9

Recycling programs for this product may not exist in your area.

THE SHEIK AND THE BOUGHT BRIDE

Visit Silhouette Books at www.eHarlequin.com

Printed in U.S.A.

Books by Susan Mallery

SUSAN MALLERY

is a *New York Times* bestselling author of more than ninety romances. Her combination of humor, emotion and just-plain-sexy has made her a reader favorite. Susan makes her home in the Pacific Northwest with her handsome husband and possibly the world's cutest dog. Visit her Web site at www.SusanMallery.com.

To my editor, Susan Litman,
who let me write the book of my heart.

Chapter One

When Victoria McCallan woke to find five armed and burly palace guards standing around her bed, she had a feeling this might not turn out to be her best day.

She was more curious than concerned about the intrusion, mostly because she hadn't done anything wrong. Well, unless she counted the extra brownie she'd had at lunch, not that anyone but her would care about her skirts getting tighter. So this had to be a mistake.

Careful to keep the sheet pulled to her shoulders, she sat up and turned on the lamp on the nightstand, then blinked in the sudden brightness.

Yup, burly guards, in uniform. She frowned as she noticed their hands seemed to be hovering by their side arms. *That* couldn't be good.

She cleared her throat and looked at the guy with the most ribbons on his jacket. "Are you sure you have the right room?" she asked.

"Victoria McCallan?"

Damn. Curiosity and concern flowed away, leaving a good dose of fear in their place.

Not that she would let the guards know. She'd always been good at acting as if everything was perfect, even as her world crumbled around her.

She raised her chin and did her best to speak without letting them see she was shaking. "That's right. How can I help you?"

"Prince Kateb would like to see you right away."

"Prince Kateb?"

She'd met him, of course. As personal assistant to Prince Nadim, she knew all the members of the royal family. Kateb rarely came into town, preferring to live in the desert. Much to the annoyance of his father.

"What does he want with me?"

"That is not for me to say. If you'll come with us?"

The guard might be asking a question, but she had a feeling she wasn't going to be allowed to say no.

"Of course. If you'll just give me a moment and some privacy to get dressed, I'll—"

"That won't be necessary," the guard told her. He tossed her the robe from the foot of the bed, then motioned for the other guards to turn around.

Victoria blinked at him. "I'm not meeting the prince in my robe."

The head guard's steely gaze told her that she just might have that one wrong.

What was going on? she wondered, as she pulled on the silk robe and then scrambled to her feet. She jerked the fabric closed and fastened the tie before slipping into her matching, lavender marabou slippers.

"This is crazy," she muttered, as much to herself as to him. "I haven't done anything wrong."

She was a good assistant, who kept track of Prince Nadim's appointments and made sure his office ran smoothly. She didn't have parties in her room or run off with the royal silver. Her passport was up-to-date, she was friendly with the other palace employees and she paid her taxes. What on earth would cause Prince Kateb, whom she barely knew, to send guards to her room? There weren't any—

She came to a stop. The head guard motioned for her to keep walking, which she did, but she wasn't paying attention to where they were going. She'd figured out the problem—and it was a big one.

A month ago, in a moment of weakness, she'd e-mailed her father. She knew better, knew that getting in touch with him would be a huge mistake. Once he'd answered, it had been too late to change her mind. He'd been delighted to discover she was living in the royal palace in El Deharia and had quickly flown out for a visit.

The man had always been nothing but trouble, she thought grimly as she was taken into an elevator and the basement button pushed. Palaces didn't actually have basements…they had dungeons. She knew enough about El Deharian history to know that nothing good ever happened in the dungeon.

The doors opened onto a long corridor. But this wasn't just any corridor. The walls were stone, and there were actual torches in iron holders, although the light came from wired fixtures on the ceiling. The place was cool and the air had a heaviness that spoke of centuries gone by and of fear.

Victoria shivered slightly and wished she'd brought a blanket to wrap around herself as well as her robe. Her high-heeled, feather-covered slippers clicked loudly on the worn stone floor. She kept her gaze firmly on the guard in front of her. His back was much safer than anything else she might see. She was terrified that ancient whips and torture devices could lie behind closed doors. She braced herself for the sound of screams and hoped if she heard any, they wouldn't be her own.

Anxiety caused her throat to tighten and made it difficult to breathe. Her father had done something bad. She was sure of it. The only question was how bad and how would the consequences affect her...again.

The guard led her to an open door, then motioned for her to go inside. She squared her shoulders, sucked in a breath she hoped wouldn't be her last and stepped into the room.

Surprisingly, the space wasn't all that scary. It was larger than she would have expected with tapestries on the wall. A carved gaming table sat in the middle and there were a half dozen or so chairs that—

Her gaze returned to the gaming table covered with playing cards, then scanned the area until she found her father standing in a corner, obviously trying to look casual.

One look at Dean McCallan told her the truth. Her charming, handsome, gambler of a father had broken his promise to never play cards again.

He was pale under his tan. His too-long blond hair no longer looked stylish. He'd gone from successful man of the world to frightened failure in the space of an evening.

"What did you do?" she asked, not caring there were other people in the room. She had to know how bad things were going to get.

"Nothing, Vi. You need to believe me." He held up both hands, as if to show his innocence. "It was a friendly game of poker."

"You weren't supposed to be playing cards. You said you were in recovery. That you hadn't played in three years."

Dean flashed her his famous smile, the one that had always made her mother weak at the knees. It triggered the opposite reaction in Victoria. She knew to brace herself because bad times were coming.

"The prince offered me a game. It would have been rude to say no."

Right. Because it couldn't be Dean's fault, she thought bitterly. There was no way her charming father would ever think to say, "Hey, Your Royal Highness, thanks for the invite but I'm not a good bet. Actually I'm too good a bet. Show me a deck of cards and I'll happily lose myself in any game. I'll also take the rent money, the food money and any savings my wife might have scraped together."

Victoria shook off the past. Her mother had died nearly ten years ago, mostly from the broken heart caused by loving Dean McCallan. She hadn't seen her father since the funeral and now she was sorry she'd ever gotten in touch with him.

"How much?" she asked knowing she would have to clean out her savings and very possibly her I.R.A. to make this right.

Dean glanced at the guards, then gave her a friendly smile. "It's not exactly about the money, Vi."

Her stomach knotted as cold fear swept through her. "Tell me you didn't cheat," she whispered, knowing if he had, it would have pushed him past saving.

There were footsteps in the corridor. Victoria turned and saw Prince Kateb sweep into the room.

She might be wearing four-inch heels, but he was still considerably taller. His eyes were dark, as was his hair, and there was a vicious scar along one cheek. The end of it just kissed the corner of his mouth, pulling it down and making him seem as if he were contemptuous of everything. Of course, that might not be the scar.

He wore dark trousers and a white shirt. Practically

casual clothes, but on him they appeared regal somehow. Without the scar, he would have been handsome. With it, he was a child's nightmare come to life. Victoria had to consciously keep from shivering in his presence.

"This is your father?" Kateb said, staring at Victoria.

"Yes."

"You invited him to visit you?"

She thought about saying she was sorry. That she hadn't seen her father in years, and he'd sworn he'd changed. She'd been stupid enough to believe him.

"Yes."

Kateb's dark gaze seemed to see through to her soul. She pulled her robe more tightly around her body, wishing the fabric was something more substantial than silk. Why couldn't she have a chenille robe like normal people? And sweats. She should be wearing sweats instead of a short nightie with cute matching panties. Not that Kateb would care about her fashion sense.

"He cheated at cards," Kateb said.

Victoria wasn't even surprised. She didn't bother looking at her father. He would say or do anything to try to make the situation better. The truth would only be a happy accident.

She raised her chin. "I apologize, sir," she said. "I assume you'll be deporting him immediately. Is it possible for me to reimburse you for the money he tried to take?"

Kateb took a step closer. "Deportation isn't enough punishment for his crime, Ms. McCallan. He has dishonored me and by doing so has dishonored the royal family of El Deharia."

"Wh-what does that mean?" Dean asked, his voice shaking. "Vi, you can't let them hurt me."

Victoria ignored him. Her mind raced. Hiring a lawyer wasn't a quick option. She would have to find one willing to take her father's case. And as it was against the royal family, that could be a trick. There was always the American embassy, but they tended to frown on U.S. citizens breaking local laws. Especially when breaking those laws insulted princes of friendly countries.

"When his dishonestly was discovered," Kateb continued, staring into Victoria's eyes as if to impress the seriousness of the situation upon her, "he didn't have the money to cover his debts."

Why would he bother, she thought bitterly. Dean had never been a fan of being responsible.

"As I said, sir, I'll cover his debts."

Kateb seemed unimpressed. "He offered something else, instead."

Victoria didn't understand. "What could my father possibly have that would be of interest to you? Whatever he's been telling you, he's not a rich man. Please. Let me pay the money he owes you. I have it in the Central Bank. I can get the account number right now and you can confirm I'm—"

"He offered you."

The room began to spin, and Victoria put out a hand to steady herself. She felt the cool, smooth stone of the wall and wished she could sink into it.

"I don't understand," she whispered.

Kateb shrugged. "When I confronted your father with his cheating, he begged me to be merciful. He offered me money, which I'm sure he did not have. When that didn't work, he said he had a beautiful daughter here in the palace who would do anything to save him. He said I could have you for as long as I wished."

Victoria straightened, then turned to stare at Dean. Her father sagged a little.

"Honey," he began, "I didn't have a choice."

"You always have a choice," she said coldly. "You could have not played cards."

The sense of betrayal was familiar, as was the disappointing realization that Dean wasn't like other fathers. Nothing mattered more than the thrill of gambling. No matter how often he promised or went to meetings or said all the right things, in the end, the cards won.

She forced herself to stand tall and face the prince. "What happens now?"

"Your father goes to prison. It will be up to the judge to determine the sentence. Eight or ten years should suffice."

"Dear God, no!" Dean McCallan sank onto the stone floor and covered his face with his hands.

He looked broken and defeated. She wanted to believe he finally understood that his actions had consequences, that he'd learned his lesson, that he would change. But she knew better. He was probably incapable of being different. It was time to turn her back on him.

Except she'd made a promise ten years ago. As her mother lay dying, she had made Victoria swear she would protect Dean, no matter what—at any cost. And Victoria had agreed—because her mother had always been there for her, had always loved her and supported her. Dean had been her only weakness and wasn't everyone allowed a single mistake?

"Punish me instead," she said, turning back to Kateb. "Let him go and take me."

Dean scrambled to his feet. "Victoria," he said, sounding hopeful, "you'd do that for me?"

"No. I'd do it for Mom." She stared at the prince. "Put me in jail. I'm a McCallan as well. The shame and dishonor is as much mine."

"I have no desire to imprison you," Kateb said, wishing

he were back in the desert, where life was simple and rules enforced without thought. Had Dean McCallan been caught cheating out there, someone would have cut off his hand…or his head. There would not be endless discussion of the problem and various solutions.

Send a woman to prison for her father's crimes? Impossible. Not even this woman who was nothing but a waste of space.

He knew Victoria McCallan—at least as much as was necessary to understand her character. She was pretty enough, in an obvious way, with impressive curves and blond hair. She worked for Prince Nadim as his assistant and had spent the past two years trying to get Nadim to notice her. She wanted to marry a prince. She cared nothing for Nadim, not that he could blame her for that. Nadim had the emotional depth of a grain of sand and the personality of gray paint. Still, Victoria had pursued him. Not that he had noticed.

Nadim's recent engagement to a woman of the king's choosing had shattered her plans. Kateb was sure that Victoria would soon be leaving their country in search of other potential rich husbands. In the meantime, there was the problem of what to do with her father.

He looked at the head guard. "Take him away."

Victoria sucked in her breath, then grabbed Kateb's arm. He ignored his body's reaction to her touch. She was female, he was male—it meant nothing more than that.

"No. You can't." She stared at him. "Please. I'll do anything."

He shook off her hand and her claim. "You exceed your position and try my patience."

"He's my father."

Kateb looked between her and the other man. He would have sworn Victoria had nothing but contempt for her father, so why this display of emotion? Why would she care? Unless the situation with Dean wasn't the main point at all. Did she see this moment as an opportunity? Was one prince as good as another?

There was a time when he had not been so cynical about women. When he had believed in love and marriage and a happy union. But he had spent the past five years being pursued by women on every continent. They didn't care about him directly—they wanted the title and the wealth that came with marrying a sheik. Nothing more.

He stepped back and looked at the woman before him. She was dressed in silk and lace, and ridiculous slippers. Her long, curly hair, large eyes and red lips were all designed to seduce. Where her robe gaped open, he could see full breasts that quivered with every breath.

She would do whatever was necessary to get what she wanted. And while he respected an adversary who would use any means to win, he didn't like those tactics being used on him.

Did she really think he was foolish enough to fall for her superficial beauty? How far would she go in her pursuit of a prince?

He looked at the father who stood anxiously awaiting the next move in the game. The man who should be defending his child, yet did nothing. Would Dean allow his daughter to sacrifice herself on his behalf, or was he in on the scam as well? Had they conspired to set up Kateb?

His gut told him they had not, but until he was sure, he would assume the worst.

"Take him into the hallway and keep him there," Kateb said, his voice low.

The guards grabbed Dean, who whimpered and pleaded, and dragged him out. The door closed behind him.

"What will you do to save your father?" he asked.

"Whatever you ask."

Something flickered in her blue eyes. Had he been a kinder man, he would have assumed fear. But he hadn't been kind for many years now.

"It must be difficult for you, a woman alone, to make her way in a man's world," he said, ignoring the growing need pounding through his body. Even disheveled and taken from her bed, she appealed to him. "The equality you took for granted in America is more difficult to find here. Yet you have done well. You've been Nadim's assistant for some time now."

"Two years."

"A pity about his engagement."

"He seems very happy."

"But you are not. All your plans…crushed."

Her spine stiffened. She stared him in the eye. "That has *nothing* to do with my father."

"Are you so sure? Perhaps you are eager to try to win me instead. What an excellent opportunity this must be for you. To present yourself dressed as you are? To beg?"

She folded her arms across her chest. "I'm dressed like this because your guards wouldn't let me put on regular clothes."

"And this is how you sleep each night? I think not."

"Then you need to go check my closet." Anger added force to her voice. "You think I'm trying to seduce you? That when I woke up and saw five guards standing around my bed I thought it was my lucky day? Oh, goody. Now I get a shot at Prince Kateb? And then they stood there while I flipped through my wardrobe and found something appropriate?"

She dropped her arms to her side. "No, wait. I know. I actually dress like this every night hoping my father, whom I haven't seen in years, happens to come by where he gets in a card game with you so he can cheat and then you send for me. Thank goodness all my plans are finally working out."

She had a point, he thought grudgingly. Not that he would admit that to her. And she had spirit, which appealed to him nearly as much as her body.

"Do you deny you wished to marry Nadim?" he demanded.

The fight seemed to go out of her. "I wouldn't have said no," she admitted, staring at the floor. "But it's not what you think. It was about security. Princes don't get divorced. At least not here."

"But you have no feelings for him."

"He's very nice."

Kateb waited.

She raised her head and glared at him. "What do you want from me? Am I to be punished because I fantasized about marrying a prince? Fine. Do what you want. You have all the power here. Right now I'm more concerned about my father."

"Why?"

"Because he's my father."

"That isn't the reason. I saw how you looked at him. You resent him for putting you in this position. You are angry with him."

"He's still my father."

Kateb allowed the silence to weigh on her. She stood her ground, meeting his gaze, not speaking. Whatever else there was, she would not tell him. Interesting.

"Will you take his place?" he asked softly.

"Yes."

"In jail?"

She swallowed. He could smell her fear.

"Yes."

"Life there is harsh. Unpleasant."

"I made a promise."

The words seemed forced out of her. He knew he had won something important but couldn't say what.

A promise. What did a woman like her know about promises?

He stared into her eyes and saw a lifetime of weariness there. Her soul was old beyond her years. Or was he simply looking for a reason because that appealed to him more than the reality of a mercenary woman taking advantage of the situation?

If only Cantara were here, with him. She would know the truth. But if she were still here, he would not be in this situation. He would not need a night of cards to fill his hours. He would not have to face the darkness that surrounded him. The emptiness.

"Your father attempted to steal from me," Kateb said coldly. "Had I not caught him cheating, he would have left this place with several hundred thousand dollars."

Victoria's breath caught.

"He cheated in the royal palace, with guards in the room. Now that there are consequences, he is content to let you take his place in prison."

"I know."

What kind of father did that? Why wasn't the man willing to be responsible? Why was she enabling his cowardice?

He wanted to teach them both a lesson. The obvious solution was to put Dean McCallan in jail.

"Return to your room," he told her. "You will be notified when he is sentenced. You will be able to visit with him before he begins serving his time, but not after. There are—"

"No!" She grabbed his arm with both hands. "No. You

can't. Please. I'll do anything." Tears filled her eyes. "My mother made me promise I would take care of him. That I wouldn't let anything bad happen to him. She died loving him. Please, I beg you. Don't lock him away. Take me instead. He offered me in the game. Did you tell him no or did you accept? Was I in play? Did you win me?"

Kateb narrowed his gaze. "I knew he didn't mean it."

"You've spoken with him. You know he did. You took the bet. You played the hand. You won me. So take me instead."

"As what?"

Victoria drew herself up to her full height. "As whatever you want."

Chapter Two

Victoria sensed Kateb's impatience with both her and the situation. She knew she was running out of options. Desperate times and all that, she thought grimly, then shrugged out of her robe.

The silk fell to the stone floor and puddled at her feet. Kateb's gaze never left her face.

"Perhaps you're not as tempting as you think," he said coolly.

"Perhaps not, but I have to try."

"You are offering yourself? For a night? Do you really think that could repay your father's transgressions?"

"I only have myself to offer." She felt cold and thought she might throw up. "You won't take my money and I have no other skills you'd appreciate. I doubt my computer skills are of much use to you in the desert." Her throat tightened and she fought fear. "It doesn't have to be for a night."

One eyebrow raised. "Longer? To what end? You are not worthy of marriage."

A well-placed slap, she thought, refusing to let him know he'd hurt her. "I will be your mistress for however long you wish. I'll go with you into the desert and do whatever you say. Anything. In return my father goes free. You can banish him from the country. Make sure he never returns to El Deharia. Just don't put him in jail."

Kateb's dark gaze continued to study her. She trembled but was determined not to let him see. At last he reached for the skinny straps on her nightie. He slid first one then the other off her shoulders. The short gown joined the robe on the stone floor.

Except for a pair of tiny bikini panties, she was naked before him. She desperately wanted to cover herself, to turn away. Embarrassment burned her cheeks, but she continued to stand there. It was the last card in her hand. If this didn't work, she would have to fold.

Dean McCallan wasn't worth it—she was clear on that. But this wasn't about him. This was about the promise she'd made her mother.

He looked her up and down. She had no idea what he was thinking—if he wanted her or not. Then he turned away.

"Cover yourself."

She had lost.

There was nothing left, she thought, refusing to cry in front of him.

Kateb stepped into the hall. Not knowing what else to do, she followed him. He stopped in front of Dean.

"Your daughter has agreed to be my mistress for six months. I will take her into the desert with me until the time is up. Then she may return. You will leave El Deharia on the first flight out in the morning. You are never to step foot in this country again. If you do, you will be shot on sight. Do I make myself clear?"

For the second time that night Victoria had trouble maintaining her balance. He was accepting? Her father wouldn't go to jail?

Momentary relief was followed by the realization that she'd, in essence, sold herself to a man she didn't know and who obviously thought very little of her.

The guard released her father. Dean grabbed Kateb's hand and shook it. "Of course. Of course. Good of you to see it was all a misunderstanding." He turned to Victoria and actually smiled at her. "I guess I need to be going. That's all right. I have business back home. Places to go. People to see."

Victoria wasn't even surprised. It was as if he hadn't heard anything except he was free to go. Nothing else mattered.

Kateb glared at him. "Did you not hear me? I'm keeping your daughter."

Dean struggled. "She's a pretty girl."

Victoria felt Kateb's fury. As a man of the desert, he would hold the protection of his family above all. That a father could give up his daughter to save himself was beyond anything he could imagine.

She quickly stepped between them. She turned her back on her father and stared into Kateb's angry, dark eyes.

"He's not worth it," she whispered. "Have the guards take him away."

"No tender goodbyes?" he asked cynically.

"What would you have to say to him if you were me?"

Kateb nodded. "Very well. Escort Mr. McCallan to his room. Guard him while he packs his things, then take him to the airport."

Victoria turned and watched her father being led away. When he reached the corner, he glanced back and waved. "I'm sure you'll be fine, Vi. Call me when you're back home."

She ignored him.

Then she and the prince of the desert were alone.

"We will also leave in the morning," he told her. "Be ready by ten."

There was an odd taste in her mouth. She supposed it was a combination of fear and apprehension.

"What should I bring?" she asked.

"Whatever you like. You will be with me for six months."

She wanted him to tell her that it would be all right. That he wasn't horrible and the time would go quickly. But she was nothing to him. Why would he offer comfort?

"You may return to your room," he told her.

She nodded and went in the opposite direction of the guards and her father. The walk to the elevator would be longer, but she wouldn't have to worry about running into them.

She had gone halfway down the hall when Kateb called to her.

She looked over her shoulder.

"The promise?" he asked. "Was he worth it?"

"Not to me," she admitted. "But he was to her."

Victoria had worried she might have trouble being ready on time, but it turned out not to be an issue. The whole not-sleeping thing really helped with time management, she thought as she checked her drawers one last time. There was nothing like a run-in with a guard and a prince, not to mention the worry of being a stranger's mistress, to keep one tense and awake. Now if only the stress took away her appetite, she could finally lose ten pounds.

She'd had no idea what to pack for six months in the desert. Nor did she know what would happen when her time with Kateb was finished. She knew she wouldn't have a job to return to. Nadim wasn't the type to hold the position open, assuming he would be interested in Kateb's former mistress as office staff. No doubt Nadim would replace her quickly and then forget she'd ever worked for him.

To think she'd spent two years trying to get her boss to notice her. Not that she'd ever been in love with him, or even sure she'd liked him. From what she'd seen, he'd been a little lacking in the personality department. But he'd represented safety and security and after the way she'd grown up, both were very appealing.

Now she had neither, she thought as she sealed the last of the boxes she was leaving behind, then pushed away the fear that made it difficult to breathe. It was only six months. Then she would return to the United States and start over. She had her savings. She would start a business of some kind, make a life. She was resourceful.

At exactly 9:58 a.m., she heard people in the hallway. She'd already sorted her luggage—the suitcases held what she would bring into the desert and the boxes contained everything else. There was an impressive pile of both. She'd accumulated a lot in the past two years.

There was a sharp knock, then Kateb swept into the room.

There was no other way to describe his appearance. He moved quickly, confidently, with a masculine grace that spoke of a man comfortable in any situation. She'd thought he might wear traditional robes for their travel but instead he had on jeans, boots and a long-sleeved shirt. If not for the air of imperial arrogance, he could almost pass for a regular kind of guy—a very handsome regular guy with that wicked scar and dark eyes that made her wonder if he could see right into her.

"You are ready?" he asked.

She motioned to the boxes and closed suitcases. "No. I just stacked these here for show."

One eyebrow raised.

Okay. Perhaps snarky humor wasn't his thing. "Sorry," she muttered. "I'm nervous. Yes, I'm ready."

"You did not try to escape in the night."

She noticed the use of the word *try*. As in "you can try, but you will fail."

"I gave my word," she said, then held up her hand. "Don't say anything bad, please. My word has value. I don't expect you to believe that, but it's true."

"Because your father's does not?"

"I know, I know. Classic psychological response to living with a chronic liar. Can we go now?"

The other eyebrow went up. Note to self: Prince Kateb didn't like snarky humor *or* someone else making the rules. Neither was especially good news, she thought.

Kateb said something she couldn't hear and several men crowded into her quarters. They reached for the luggage and the boxes.

"I'm taking those with me," she said, indicating the bags. "The boxes will be stored." She gave the floor and room number of where they should be taken.

Kateb nodded, as if his permission were required for them to do as she said. And it probably was.

"Is there electricity where we're going?" she asked. "I brought my curling iron." Not to mention her blow-dryer, her iPod and her cell-phone charger. She wasn't sure about cell service out in the desert, but she would want to charge it before she returned to the city.

"Once we arrive, you will have everything that you need," he told her.

Which, she noted, wasn't exactly a *yes*. "I'm guessing we have different ideas about what I need. You are unlikely to see the importance of a curling iron."

His gaze moved to her hair, which she'd pulled back in

a ponytail for the trip. But she'd still curled the ends. She might be going to the girlfriend equivalent of prison, but she would look good on the way.

"We will leave now," he told her.

She followed him out of the room and into the corridor. There was no one to see her off. Her friend, Maggie, was on a trip with her fiancé, Prince Oadir—Kateb's brother. Victoria had left a note explaining she would be gone for a while. After two years in El Deharia, she didn't have any friends back home who would notice she'd disappeared for a few months, and she certainly wasn't going to be in touch with her father. It was, she thought sadly, a very lonely feeling.

They walked through the palace, heading for the back. When they stepped outside Victoria saw several large trucks in the rear courtyard.

"I don't have *that* much luggage," she said, wondering what they were for.

"We are taking supplies," Kateb told her. "The desert people trade for what they need. You will travel with me." He pointed to a Land Rover parked on the side.

"The SUV of kings," she murmured. Didn't the British royal family also use Land Rovers? But she didn't ask. Speaking suddenly seemed difficult. Despite the bright sun and warm temperature, her body felt stiff and cold. The closer she got to the SUV, the harder it was to move. Fear clawed at her throat. Panic made her stomach clench.

She couldn't do this. Couldn't go out in the desert with a man she didn't know. What was going to happen? How horrible was it going to be? Her father didn't deserve her sacrifice, she thought bitterly. He certainly didn't appreciate it.

But she hadn't done it for her father, she reminded herself.

"Victoria?"

A guard held open the passenger door. She sucked in a steadying breath and slid onto the smooth leather. The car door closed next to her. The sound seemed unnaturally loud—as if she'd just been cut off from everything safe and good.

Her luggage had already been loaded into one of the trucks. She was the only woman in a sea of workers and guards and drivers. There was no one to appeal to, no one to protect her. She was truly on her own.

Kateb drove the familiar road into the desert. For the first day, they would see signs of villages and small towns but by this time tomorrow, all civilization would have been left behind.

Victoria was mercifully silent. After a restless night, he wasn't in the mood for inane conversation. Under normal circumstances he wouldn't have blamed her for his lack of sleep, but he'd spent the hours of darkness tossing and turning in his bed, trying not to think about her. An impossible task, given that he'd seen her nearly naked the day before.

It was as if the image of her body were imprinted on his brain. He didn't have to close his eyes to see her pale skin and full breasts. The vision taunted him, reminding him how long it had been since he'd been with a woman. And the wanting made him angry.

He knew the anger was more about himself than her, but she was easy to blame. If he'd had less self-control, he would have pulled over and taken her right there, on the front seat, the men with them be damned. But he wouldn't. Not only because he would never force her or put on a show for his men, but because the need was too specific. He wanted Victoria, not a faceless woman to satisfy himself, and that bothered him.

It had been five years since Cantara had died. Five years during which he'd mourned her loss. There had been times when desire had driven him to someone's bed, but those brief hours had been about physical need. The woman herself had been a means to an end. Nothing more. He refused to have Victoria be different.

She was nothing like Cantara. His beautiful wife had been desert born, a laughing, dark-haired beauty. They'd grown up together. He'd known everything about her. There had been no surprises, no mysteries, and he preferred that. She had understood him, his position, his destiny. She had been proud, but never assumed they were equals. She had been his wife and that had been enough for her.

He glanced at Victoria, taking in the perfect profile, the fullness of her mouth. This woman would not be content to be anything but a man's true match, he thought. She would expect her opinion to matter. She would want to *talk* about everything. Her feelings, her plans, her life. It was more than a prince should have to bear. She would—

He glanced at her again and noticed the slight tremor in her cheek. As if her teeth had been tightly clenched for some time. She was pale and had her hands tightly clasped. He caught it then, the bitter scent.

Fear.

The knowledge made him weary. He was not cruel enough to allow her to terrorize herself with her concerns.

"Nothing will happen until we arrive at the village," he said sharply.

Her breath caught. He felt her glance at him. "H-how long will that take?"

"Three days. Very few people know the place. It's beautiful, at least I find it so. Like nothing you've ever seen."

He hoped she wouldn't ask what would happen when they did finally arrive. He had no answer for that. He had taken her because she had offered herself in exchange for her father and the desert law respected a noble sacrifice.

But to what end? Did he really plan to take her for his mistress?

He looked at her again. She wore jeans and ridiculous boots with high heels. The shirt was made of some clingy fabric that seemed to hug her breasts. He forced himself to return his attention to the road.

He found her attractive and would enjoy her in his bed, but he was reluctant to commit to longer than a single night. Which meant he was going to have to find something else for Victoria to do.

"I, uh, thought the people of the desert were nomadic," she said.

"Many are, but many also enjoy life in the desert and do not feel compelled to move from camp to camp. The village provides the best of both worlds."

"I hope I brought enough sunscreen," she murmured.

"We will send for more if you did not," he told her.

"So you don't plan to stake me out in the sun and let the ants eat me alive?"

"This is not the Old West," said Kateb, bemused.

"I know, but it's still a pretty gruesome punishment. Hanging would be faster."

"There is less opportunity for a rescue with a hanging."

"Good point."

The fear had faded. Now he could smell her perfume, or maybe just the scent of her body. Either way it pleased him and in being pleased, he was annoyed.

Kateb sighed. It was going to be a long six months.

They made two brief stops for water and bathroom breaks. Victoria was thrilled they used something very close to a rest area, although she had a bad feeling the amenities were going to get worse before they got better.

Just before sunset they stopped for the night and made

camp. Several tents were put up along with what looked like sleeping bags and bedrolls. Two men went to work over a large camp stove while another set up something that looked suspiciously like a gas barbecue.

Kateb came up beside her. "You look concerned. Are the facilities not to your liking?"

She guessed he was seeking information rather than offering to change anything on her behalf. She pointed at the stove. "I thought there would be an open fire and we'd be cooking food on sticks."

That single eyebrow raised again. "Where would we get fuel for the fire?"

She glanced around at the campsite. They'd backed in the trucks, butting them up against a cliff. There were a few sad-looking shrubs, but nothing that could pass for logs or even sticks.

"True."

"The stoves are more efficient. They heat quickly and there is little danger from fire."

"There's not that much to burn."

"There is us."

"Oh. Right." She looked at the men working quickly by the stove. "Should I offer to help? At the castle the chefs were very fussy about who they allowed in their kitchen. They let me rinse off berries once." Which she'd apparently done incorrectly because one of the cooks had muttered something under his breath and grabbed the basket from her.

"Why would you help?"

"They're staff, I'm staff. It's polite to offer."

"You are not expected to cook the meal."

Right. Because she was expected to provide other services. Her stomach tightened, which she ignored, along with any thoughts about sharing Kateb's bed. That was for later. When they arrived at the mysterious desert village. For now she was safe.

She glanced at him, at the proud set of his head, at the deep scar on his cheek. Kateb ruled the desert. He could do what he would like with her and no one would stop him. Which made *safe* a relative term. She took a step back.

"I've never been camping," she said. "This is nice. Desert life is more modern than I would have thought."

"This is not desert life. This is efficient transportation. To be in the desert is to be one with the land. It is to travel with camels and horses, bringing only what you need, knowing what you forget you do without. There is beauty deep in the desert, but danger as well."

Her gaze was drawn to his scar. She'd heard rumors that he'd been attacked as a teenager, but she never learned the details. Asking hadn't seemed important. Her total knowledge about Kateb would barely fill a good-sized e-mail. If she'd known she was going to be spending some serious time in his company, she would have asked more questions.

One of the men brought over two folding chairs, setting them in the shade. Victoria wasn't sure of protocol, but she waited until Kateb was seated before sitting down herself. When the man returned with two bottles of water, she accepted one gratefully.

"I grew up in Texas," she said, more to fill the silence than because she thought he was interested. "A little town between Houston and Dallas. It was nothing like this, although it could get hot in the summer. There weren't a lot of trees, so when people were outside, there wasn't anywhere to go to escape the sun. I remember summer storms racing through. I would stand out in the rain, spinning and spinning. Not that the rain cooled things off very much."

"Did you like living there?"

"I didn't know anything else. My dad would disappear for weeks at a time. Mom missed him when he was gone, but I liked that it was just the two of us. It felt safer. Then he would come back, sometime with a lot of money, sometimes broke and driving on fumes. Either way she was happy—until he left again."

That was a long time ago, she thought sadly. But she remembered everything about those days.

"When did she die?"

"On my seventeenth birthday."

Victoria didn't want to think about that. "She worked two jobs most of the time. She did hair during the day and worked at a bar at night. She used to talk about us opening a beauty shop together. I never wanted to tell her that I was just waiting to turn eighteen to leave."

"Where did you go?"

"Dallas." She smiled at the memory. "It was really the big city for me. I got a job, enrolled in community college and worked my butt off. I started off waitressing at a diner, then moved up to nicer places. I made a lot with tips and when I got my associates degree, I found a job as an administrative assistant."

"Why not a four-year degree?"

"Have you priced college lately?" She shrugged. "It's a lot more money. Working full-time and going to college isn't easy. So I got a job working for an oil company."

"And through them, met Nadim."

She could hear the judgment in his voice. "Eventually."

"What about your father?"

"I didn't talk to him much. He came by a few times, looking for money."

"Did you give him any?"

"The first time. Then I stopped." She didn't want to

think about that, either. "So there's probably not a shower in one of those trucks."

"No. You will have to wait until we arrive at the village."

Great. "And I'm going to go out on a limb and say you didn't think to bring an extension cord. For my curling iron?"

He stared at her. There wasn't a hint of humor in his dark eyes or even a twitch of his mouth. "No."

"You don't actually do the humor thing, do you?" she asked, knowing it was probably a mistake, or at least presumptuous.

"Were you being funny?"

She laughed. "Careful. You wouldn't want to appear human."

"I am many things, Victoria."

His gaze was steady as he spoke. Steady and almost… predatory.

No, she told herself. She was imagining things. He wasn't actually interested in her. Keeping her around was all about her paying her father's debt. But once the idea appeared in her brain, she couldn't seem to push it away. It made her aware of him, sitting close to her. Of the way he dominated the space, despite the fact that they were outdoors.

She shivered.

"Do we, um, drive the whole way?" she asked, hoping a neutral topic change would make her feel better.

"Not quite." He looked away. "There is a road to the village. The last day I will ride. You may join me if you wish. Assuming you ride."

"Horses, right? Not camels."

"No camels."

"Then I ride." She'd learned the first year she'd been in El Deharia. Having access to the royal stable was one of the perks of her job. Even the lesser horses the staff was permitted to ride were still amazing, purebred animals that ran like the wind.

"I hope you have more sensible boots than those."

She glanced down at her fashionable boots with their four-inch heels. "These are stunning."

"They are impractical."

"They were on sale. You would seriously die if I told you how much I'd saved." She looked at him, then away. "Or maybe not." Something told her Kateb wasn't the type to shop. Or care about a sale.

She heard a sharp cry in the distance. A louder call answered nearby. Whatever made it sounded large and wolflike.

Her instinct was to run for safety, but Kateb didn't move and none of the other men reacted.

"Is that something we should worry about?" she asked.

"Not if you stay close to camp."

Suddenly their location seemed more thought-out than she'd first thought. With the cliffs at their back and the trucks forming a semicircle, it would be difficult for someone to attack from any direction.

While she appreciated the planning, she hoped it wasn't a necessary precaution. If they were attacked, she wouldn't be good for much more than shrieking panic.

What on earth was she doing here, in the middle of the desert with a man she didn't know? What had she been thinking, throwing herself on Kateb's mercy and offering to take her father's place? Dean had earned some time in jail. He'd cheated at cards and offered her as payment. She shouldn't care what happened to him.

Only she hadn't done it for him, she reminded herself.

She looked at Kateb, wondering what he expected of her. What would he want her to do? Did he really plan to take her to his bed? Fear claimed her, making it difficult not to bolt for freedom. Not that the desert provided much more safety.

"Is one of those tents mine?" she asked.

He pointed to the one in the middle.

"Excuse me," she said, and walked toward it.

Inside she found a cot with bedding. Her luggage had been piled against the other cloth wall. She supposed by tent standards, it was very nice. There was certainly enough room.

But she didn't care about any of that. Instead she sank onto the cot, then rolled onto her side and curled up in a ball. The unknown loomed like a circling vulture, ready to pick her bones clean.

She sniffed. Okay, that was a bit melodramatic, but she was scared. Down-to-the-core terrified.

Outside she heard the men talking. A while later, the tent flap opened and one of the cooks told her that dinner was ready.

"Thank you," she said as she pushed up on her elbow. "I'm not hungry."

He said something she didn't understand and backed out of the tent. Seconds later Kateb stalked in.

"What is your problem?" he demanded.

"I'm not hungry."

"Are you pouting? I will not tolerate an emotional tantrum. You will get up and come and eat."

His obvious contempt drove her to her feet. She put her hands on her hips and glared at him.

"You don't get to judge me," she snapped. "I'm having a really bad day, okay? I'm sorry if that reality upsets you, but you're going to have to deal with it."

"I have no idea what you're talking about."

"Sure you do. You think I'm trash. Worse than trash, because you don't think of me at all. I'm just an…I don't know what. But from my perspective, I just sold myself to you. I don't know you from a rock and I don't know what's going to happen. I sold myself for a man who doesn't deserve it and now I'm here with you in the desert. You said I have until we get to the village. What happens there? What are you going to do to me? Are you going to…r-rape me?"

Her voice started to shake and she could feel her eyes burning, but she refused to look away or back down.

Kateb sucked in a breath. "I am Prince Kateb of El Deharia. How dare you accuse me of such things?"

"It's actually pretty damned easy. You won me in a card game and now you're dragging me into the desert to be your mistress for six months. What am I supposed to think?" She glared at him. "Don't you dare tell me not to be upset. I would think, under the circumstances, I get to be a little nervous."

He grabbed her arm. "Stop."

A single tear escaped. She wiped it away and was still.

"I will not hurt you," he said quietly.

"How do I know that?"

Their eyes locked. She wanted to see something on his face, something yielding or gentle. There was only the darkness and the sharp edges of the scar. Kateb turned and left.

She stood alone in the center of her tent, not sure what to think. Exhaustion made her sit on the edge of the cot. Now what?

Before she could figure out what to do next, he returned carrying a plate along with a bottle of water and an odd-shaped black box. It was about the size of a small loaf of bread.

"You must eat," Kateb told her, handing her the food. "You don't want to get sick."

The scent of meat and vegetables made her stomach growl, but she was too afraid to eat.

"What's that?" she asked, pointing at the box.

"A battery-pack converter." He turned it so she could see the shorter side. When he lifted the flap, there was a plug, just like a regular outlet. "For your curling iron." He set it on the floor of the tent.

She couldn't believe it. "Really? I can curl my hair?"

"You seem to find that very essential."

She was still afraid, but didn't seem so desperate now. Her stomach growled again, and she thought maybe she could eat. Answers continued to elude her, but for now, that was all right.

Chapter Three

By day three, they had settled into a routine. One Victoria found easy to deal with as it mostly involved Kateb ignoring her. While he was in the camp and occasionally spoke to her, he'd had her ride in a different vehicle and acted as if she were just one of the guys. That allowed her to relax a little and ignore their destination.

The desert had a unique beauty, she thought when they stopped for lunch. She accepted a bowl of stew from the cook and smiled her thanks. The dry air meant good hair days, although she was dying for a shower. At this point she was desperate enough to be willing to give up her favorite leather jacket for fifteen minutes of warm water and a bar of soap.

She sat in her usual place, at the back of the camp. This time there weren't cliffs behind them, but more of the trucks. While no one walked around with a rifle, she knew that the men were always aware of the surroundings. Kateb more so than any.

He watched the sky, scanned the horizon. She suspected he would be able to tell her if there was a rabbit or fox within five miles. Or something more dangerous.

She liked how he was with the other men. He commanded their respect without being pushy about it. They looked to him because he was naturally their leader.

Her gaze returned to the scar. What had happened to him? She wanted to ask, but they weren't speaking that much and it didn't seem like a good conversation starter. There was a sort of truce between them she didn't want to disrupt. Last night he'd brought her a lantern, so she could read if she wished. Not exactly the actions of a savage madman.

So maybe the mistress thing wouldn't be too horrible. He was intelligent and strong. He joked with the other men. She liked the sound of his laugh, not that he ever laughed with her.

When she finished her lunch, she carried the bowl over to the wash bucket and cleaned it. When she straightened, Kateb stood next to her.

She jumped. "Why do you have to be stealthy?"

"We are close to the village. It's less than twenty miles by horseback, although nearly fifty in the truck. The trucks require a road. I will be riding the rest of the way. Would you care to join me?"

"Sure. Thanks. Give me ten minutes to change my clothes." She glanced around. Tents weren't put up in the middle of the day, which meant privacy was an issue. Maybe she could climb in the back of one of the trucks.

"Why do you need to change your clothes? You're even wearing sensible boots."

She glanced down at her authentic cowboy boots. "I know. They're so cool. I got them on sale. But I have a riding outfit."

"Do you have different clothes for every event?"

"Of course. It's a girl thing. Although I was challenged by the whole 'you'll be my mistress.' That was a stumper. They don't cover it much in the fashion magazines. I think they're missing a real market."

He was much taller than she and had to look down to meet her gaze. "You hide your emotions behind humor," he said.

It was all she could do not to roll her eyes. "Well, duh."

One corner of his mouth twitched. An actual twitch, which was nearly a smile. She wasn't sure why making him smile or laugh would make her feel better, but she believed that all the way down to her toes.

"What you are wearing is fine," he told her.

"But the outfit is really cool."

"You can show me later."

"You just don't want to wait while I dig through all my luggage."

"There is that, as well. Be ready in five minutes."

"There aren't any horses."

"There will be."

Kateb walked away. Victoria watched him go, not sure what to make of him. On the one hand, he'd taken her for his mistress for six months and that couldn't be good. On the other hand, he'd given her electricity for her curling iron and taken care of her, albeit from a distance. Which meant this was the strangest semi-relationship she'd ever had in her life.

Four minutes and thirty seconds later, a man rode up leading two horses. Kateb spoke with him, then brought the horses to her.

"How well do you ride?" he asked.

"Isn't it a little late to be worrying about that?"

He looked at her.

So much for the lip twitch. "I do okay. I'm not an expert, but I've been riding every couple of days for nearly two years."

One of the men walked over and laced his fingers together to form a step. Victoria glanced back at the trucks holding all her things, including her purse. Was she just going to ride away and leave them all behind? Did she have a choice?

She stepped in the man's hand, pushed off the ground, then swung into the saddle. After three days of driving, it felt good to be on a horse, out in the fresh air. Kateb got on his horse and moved the animal next to hers.

"We'll be heading northeast."

"Do I look like I know what direction that is?"

He pointed out into the wilderness, toward rolling hills dotted with low shrubs and grasses growing out of the sand. Like that would help.

He urged his horse forward. Hers moved into step without her doing anything, which meant it was probably going to be an easy ride. Her favorite kind.

"If you try to escape, I won't look for you," he told her. "You'll wander for days before dying of thirst."

"Oh, please," she said, before she could remember he was royalty and sometimes it was better not to say everything she was thinking. "That's so much crap."

He didn't bother looking at her. "You think so?"

"You're not going to leave me out here to die."

"Do you want to test your certainty?"

"Probably not."

He smiled then. A real lip-moving kind of smile. His eyes crinkled at the corners, his expression relaxed. His face was transformed from unreadable and stern to approachable and handsome.

Somewhere deep inside, her stomach tightened, but this

time it had nothing to do with fear or apprehension and everything to do with the man. She felt a little tingly and light-headed. Those reactions were quickly followed by a different kind of panic.

No, no, no, she told herself. There was no way she could be attracted to Kateb. None at all. Talk about the danger zone. She knew better than to give her heart to a man. That road led only to ruin. And falling for a sheik who was going to toss her aside in six months was a whole new level of stupid.

She drew in a breath. She had to get a grip. Finding Kateb attractive didn't mean anything. It was biology. Okay—there'd been a tingle, but a tingle was a long way from love. She was completely safe. All it meant was that when he finally wanted her in his bed, the experience might not be icky. That was a good thing.

"What?" Kateb demanded. "Are you sick?"

"No. Why?"

"You look odd."

Which was probably prince-speak for "you have a strange look on your face." At least that was her assumption. Not that she was going to answer the implied question of "what were you thinking?"

Diversion seemed like a good idea. "How long have you lived in the desert?"

"Since I graduated from university."

"Why the desert?"

"When I was ten, my brothers and I spent the summer in the desert. It is a traditional for the king's sons to learn the ways of the nomads. I had always found the palace and rules constricting. For me, being in the desert was like coming home. I came back every summer, living with different tribes. One year I lived in the village and knew that was to be my home."

"You didn't want to spend all your time visiting Paris and dating supermodels?"

"I have been to Paris. It is a beautiful city. Just not for me."

"And the supermodels?"

He didn't bother answering.

The sun was hot, but not oppressive. Victoria adjusted her hat and was grateful she'd used her five minutes to slather on sunscreen.

"What do you do in the village? I can't see you selling used camels."

"I am working with the elders and business owners to develop a more stable financial infrastructure. There is plenty of capital flowing through the area, but no one is capturing it and using it effectively."

"Let me guess," she said. "You have a degree in finance."

"Yes."

"It shows."

He changed tactics. "How did you come to work for Nadim?"

"He was in Dallas for several weeks. His assistant had a medical emergency and had to fly back to El Deharia. I'd worked with his assistant and apparently got a good review. Nadim asked that I be assigned to him and when he went back, he offered me a job."

"Was it love at first sight for you?"

While there wasn't exactly a sneer in the question, there was definite tone.

"I never claimed to love him," she said primly.

"Does that make it better or worse?"

"I did my job well. Nadim had no complaints about my performance. As to the rest, arranged marriages are still a tradition in this part of the world. I was just trying to arrange my own."

"So you could be rich."

He still didn't get it.

"It's not about money."

"So you have said." He sounded as if he didn't believe her.

She looked out over the desert. She couldn't see anything resembling a village, but she wished they would get there quickly. Suddenly riding with Kateb wasn't that much fun anymore.

Annoyance bubbled inside of her until it spilled out. "You haven't got a clue," she told him. "You can't know. You grew up a prince, in privilege. You never worried about having enough to eat. You don't know what it's like to see your mom crying because there's no food for dinner because your dad took all the money. He would do that— come in and take every cent she had. Sometimes he would sell stuff, like our TV. One time he sold her car and she had to walk to work for nearly a year while she saved enough to get a down payment for a new one."

Victoria drew in a breath. "I was poor. Dirt poor. My clothes came from the church ladies who brought them by. While I appreciate their intentions, it was humiliating to be given clothes their daughters had already worn at school. To have to walk into class the next day and listen to the laughter and whispers. You've never had to stand in a different line at lunch because your food was paid for by the state and everyone knew. You don't understand what it's like to be a charity case."

She hadn't been paying attention so she hadn't noticed how big the past had grown until it overwhelmed her. The need to get away made her kick her horse, then lean forward in the saddle as the gelding raced toward the horizon.

Kateb watched her go. She was riding in the correct direction so he didn't worry about her getting lost. If she gave her horse his head, he would find his way back to the stable.

Victoria moved well in the saddle, although her shoulders were slumped forward, as if weighed down by a heavy burden.

Did she speak the truth? He didn't know her well enough to trust her word, but the shame in her eyes had been real, as had the pain in her voice. If she had grown up as poor as she said, perhaps he could understand why security was so important to her. It also explained her obsession with clothes and finding things on sale.

She rode up to the slight rise, then reined in her horse. He joined her.

"Is that the village?" she asked, surprised.

"Yes."

"You have to work on your definitions."

Victoria had imagined a few tents, a primitive barn, maybe a lean-to. What she saw instead was a thriving rural city, with streets and houses and barns and fields.

"They farm?" she asked.

"Yes. There are several underground rivers that provide irrigation. In the desert, water is life."

She couldn't take it all in. "How many people live here?"

"Several thousand."

"Hardly a village."

"It has grown."

The fields were outside the structures, stretching out along the edges of the valley and up the hills in terraces. There were several open-air markets, a larger building that could have been a church or a school. A road wound down into the valley. She could see the trucks slowly moving toward the village. At the far end of the valley, up against the cliffs, a stone structure seemed to dominate the landscape.

"What's that?" she asked, pointing toward it.

"The Winter Palace."

"Palace for whom?"

"In ancient times, the King of El Deharia would spend a few months here each year. When that stopped, the elders' council established a leader for the people. He is nominated and serves a twenty-five-year term."

She remembered hearing about that. Kateb was supposed to be on the short list for that job. "Twenty-five years is a long time. They don't want to make a mistake."

"If they do, there are ways to unseat him."

"And it always has to be a man, right?"

He flashed that killer smile again. "Of course. We are progressive, but we do not yet support the idea of a woman ruling."

"That is just so typical," she muttered. "So the leader gets the palace and all that goes with it?"

"Yes. The previous leader, Bahjat, died a few months ago, causing the new search. He graciously allowed me rooms in the palace when I was in residence."

"Because you're the king's son."

"Partially. We were close. He was like a grandfather to me."

"Then you must miss him."

Kateb nodded and started down the side of the mountain.

The trail was easier than it looked. Victoria hung on, letting her horse pick his way. She would guess he was a lot more sure-footed than she would be.

It took nearly an hour to make their way to the valley. They rode past fields and farmhouses, then moved onto a dirt path beside a paved road. She couldn't believe how big the so-called village was and how many people lived here. There was an interesting combination of old and new. Watermills nestled next to generators.

The houses were mostly stone, with big windows and thick walls. Porches provided shade. Nearly every home had a garden and pipes bringing in water.

People waved at Kateb and called out greetings. He waved back. She felt the stares and didn't know what she was supposed to do.

The relative calm of the journey faded as they approached the end of the trip. Kateb had given her a brief reprieve and it was nearly over. What was going to happen next?

"Will I be at the palace?" she asked. "Or somewhere else?"

"You will have quarters at the palace. They are separate from mine."

Okay—that was good. She could use her own space.

"Is there a shower?"

He glanced at her. Amusement brightened his eyes. "One that will satisfy even you."

How nice. But what happened after the shower? What happened that night?

"You will find electricity and many other modern improvements," he said.

She did her best to ignore the chill brought on by fear. *One step at a time*, she told herself. They would get to the palace and then she could deal with the rest of her life. For now she should just enjoy the ride.

But the ride was going to be too short, she thought, feeling the first wisps of panic curling through her.

She did her best to distract herself by studying the open-air market they passed. There were plenty of fresh fruits and vegetables for sale, along with a display of the woven gold she liked so much. Later she would come back to shop. That would make her happy. Shopping was—

They turned a corner and the Winter Palace loomed before them.

From what she could see, the palace was made up of several buildings, with the central one being the largest. It was stone, with rising towers and a formidable stone wall surrounding the grounds. The roof was tile and seemed to have an iridescent quality that glimmered in the bright sun. There was a real drawbridge in the center of the stone wall, along with several permanent bridges to the right and left. People walked back and forth through the opening.

"How will the trucks get in?" she asked.

"The road goes around back. There are garages and a delivery entrance."

Once they rode over the drawbridge, more people called to Kateb. They greeted him warmly, welcoming him back. Although they glanced at her, no one asked why she was here. Victoria didn't want to know what they were thinking. As there had been no talk of Kateb taking a new bride, they would probably guess the reason for her presence. That she was here to service the prince. It was like standing in the free-lunch line in elementary school all over again.

Kateb reined in his horse and dismounted. She had a wild urge to bolt for freedom, only to remind herself she had no idea which way to go. And as much as she was frightened of that night, it was better than a slow, dry death in the desert.

She got off her horse. It took a second for her legs to remember what it was like to walk rather than ride, then she followed Kateb into the palace.

The entryway soared up several stories. The stone walls were smooth, the windows stained glass. Sunlight created colors on the floor and people passing through the entry. Large tapestries told the history of the desert.

Victoria wanted to move closer and study them. She'd found El Deharian history fascinating and was sure it would be just as interesting to study this place.

"Is there a library?" she asked.

"Yes."

"Can I use it?"

"Of course. Come this way."

She followed Kateb down several long corridors. While there were still people everywhere, she ignored them as she took in the paintings and statues that dotted the palace. There were treasures everywhere she looked. Marble and gold. A portrait that looked eerily like a da Vinci. Not that she was much of an art expert. But wouldn't it be fun to search for the signature?

She was so caught up in the beauty of the palace that she nearly forgot why she was here. It wasn't until Kateb stopped in front of a single carved door that she remembered to be afraid.

"You will be staying here," he said as he pulled open the door. "I trust you will find your quarters comfortable."

It wasn't a question, she thought, her heart pounding hard and fast.

Beautiful rugs in a rainbow of colors muffled the sounds of their steps. She had a brief impression of oval couches and overstuffed chairs, inlaid tables and hanging lanterns.

There were many rooms, all flowing from one to the other. Everything about the space spoke of time and past lives, as if they were in the oldest part of the palace.

Kateb kept walking until they reached a walled garden. Lush plants grew everywhere. Jasmine scented the air. She saw a flash of movement as a parrot flew by.

Victoria turned in a slow circle. Her brain resisted the

information but it was hard to ignore. Many rooms. Walled gardens. Parrots.

The rooms would be required for all the residents who had once lived here. The walled gardens kept the women in and the men out. And the parrots concealed the sounds of their voices, for no one else could hear their words or their laughter. It was forbidden.

She stopped in front of Kateb, put her hands on her hips and wished she had something to throw at him.

"You brought me to the *harem*?"

"It seemed appropriate," he said, with the hint of a smile, then left.

Chapter Four

Victoria stared at the closed door of the harem, wondering if she'd heard the click of a lock, or if that was just her imagination at work. And did she really want to find out which? She supposed the good news was he hadn't taken her to his own suite, which meant she would have plenty of privacy and space. A good thing, she thought, trying to find the silver lining in what might be a very dark cloud.

She turned so she could study the huge space. Dozens of rooms all flowed into each other. There were amazing tapestries on the walls and beautiful, handmade wooden tables. She crossed to one and touched the inlaid wood. Master craftsmen, she thought. How many months had it taken for just this one piece?

Had anyone bothered to document the furniture or artwork? If not, it should be done. A history preserved. Maybe, if the library had research books that could help, she could start. Assuming she wasn't locked in here like a prisoner.

"There's only one way to find out," she murmured, as she crossed the stone floor. But before she reached the carved door, she heard footsteps.

She turned and saw a tall, older woman walking toward her. She was dressed in a flowing long dress that looked both cool and comfortable. Her gray hair had been piled on her head. Gold earrings dangled and there were dozens of bracelets on both wrists.

"You must be Victoria," she said with a smile. "I was told you were coming. Welcome to the Winter Palace. I am Yusra."

"Thank you."

"We are all excited that the harem is back in use. It has been too many months of silence in these walls."

That made Victoria take a step back. "You think trapping women inside these walls is a good thing?"

"Of course. The old ways must be preserved. Just because something is old doesn't mean it doesn't have value."

"I agree with that, but I'm missing the positive side of being locked up against one's will for the sole purpose of pleasing a man. How is that helpful to the women?"

Yusra frowned. "To be in the leader's harem is to be given a privileged life. If one was fortunate enough to bear him children, then that woman would live here forever. Even if the leader got tired of her."

"Not a great argument. Why does *he* get to say when he's tired? Why not her? What if she doesn't want to stay here? What if she wants to go out in the village and have a real husband and family?"

"Then she would go."

"Just like that?"

"Of course. There is no lock on the outside of the door, Victoria. Only one on the inside, to keep out those who don't belong. No woman has ever been kept in the Winter Palace against her will."

Until now, Victoria thought grimly. Although she wasn't here against her will. Not exactly. She'd offered herself in exchange for her father. She'd begged Kateb to take her instead.

"I'm sorry," she said. "I'm tired and everything is new and confusing. I wasn't expecting…this."

Yusra smiled again. "The harem is a beautiful place. You will find it such. There are many wonders, many things to explore. Come. I will show you."

Victoria followed her down a hallway to several sleeping rooms. There were big beds with gauzy curtains and windows that opened out onto the gardens. Beautiful ceiling fans stirred the air and handmade rugs added color to the floor.

"I took the liberty of choosing this room for you," Yusra said, entering a large space with French doors that led directly into the garden. "If you don't like it, you may choose another."

"This is very nice," Victoria said, trying not to notice the very big bed—one plenty large enough for two…or even six. Kateb was unlikely to come to the harem. While she was here, she was safe. It was only when he called for her that she had to worry. At least that's what she told herself as she felt nervous tension tightening her throat.

"Your things are here." Yusra motioned to the suitcases along the far wall. "Will you need assistance unpacking?"

"No, thanks. I can do it." After all, she'd managed to pack and unpack for herself for years now.

"I have also provided you with more traditional clothing."

Traditional as in what?

Victoria followed her into a dressing area with a large closet and several sets of drawers. Long, flowing dresses hung in the closet. She touched one of the patterned sleeves and discovered the material was silk and decorated with impossibly small stitches. Each dress was more beautiful than the next, with swirls of color and fluttering sleeves. It was only when she removed one from the hanger and held it in front of her that she realized the fabric was completely sheer.

Her thighs started to tremble. "So, um, what do I wear under something like this?"

Yusra's smile turned wicked. "Nothing at all." She laughed. "You will enjoy these. I did in my day. The beading and patterns are designed to provide a little modesty for the woman and some mystery for the man. The fabric caresses the skin, reminds her of her lover's touch. You'll see."

Too much information, Victoria thought as she quickly returned the dress to the closet. She wasn't sure why she was the one blushing, but she felt definite heat on her cheeks.

"Let me show you the bath," Yusra said. "You will need time to get ready."

Victoria ignored the implication in that statement and instead concentrated on seeing the bath. The harem baths of El Deharia were legendary. She'd heard of gold faucets and tubs as big as pools.

They crossed the hall and walked through a beaded curtain. Victoria's breath caught as she took in the open area with the stained-glass windows and skylights. The sound of a waterfall filled the air.

On either side of the door were vanities with armless upholstered chairs. The fabric looked old and she itched to find it in a book somewhere to date it. A hundred years old at least, she thought excitedly.

After passing through an archway, they moved into the main area of the bath. Yusra pointed to several doors.

"Steam shower," she said. "Sauna. Treatment room. Should you desire a massage, we have a masseuse who will come here. She is excellent. Whirlpool tub. Regular shower."

Why would anyone bother with a regular shower? Victoria stepped closer to the huge pool of swirling water. At one end was a raised rock platform with a waterfall pouring from it. The perfect outdoor shower, right here in the harem bath.

Lush plants grew at the water's edge. The spray caught the light from the stained-glass windows and created rainbows where it fell. It was paradise, right in the middle of the desert.

"Is the water warm?" she asked.

"Yes. About one hundred degrees. The spring below the palace is filtered, heated water. From here it drains through sand and rock and returns to the earth."

Perfection and environmentally friendly, Victoria thought, unable to believe this really existed.

"You will want to freshen up from your journey," Yusra told her.

"Possibly for hours."

The older woman showed her stacks of fluffy towels on shelves and several terry-cloth robes hanging on hooks. Then they returned to the main room.

"It's beautiful," Victoria admitted. While she might be nervous about the circumstances, she couldn't complain about the working conditions.

Yusra showed her a phone on a small table. "Call if you need anything. Meals will be left in the small kitchen in back. There is fresh fruit and water, as well. Tell the main kitchen what you desire and it will be provided." She looked at an antique grandfather clock. "The prince is expecting you for dinner tonight. I will send someone to escort you to his rooms in two hours."

Victoria's good mood faded. Tonight? So soon?

"We welcome you to the Winter Palace," Yusra said earnestly. "The prince has been sad for many years now."

Sad? Kateb? She hadn't noticed.

"You are the first woman he has brought here in a very long time," the older woman continued. "Perhaps you can make him smile again."

It seemed like a tall order. At this point she would accept not being terrified all the time as a win.

When Victoria was alone, she returned to the big bedroom and went through her suitcases. As she unpacked, she kept trying *not* to think about what might happen that night.

"He must be tired," she whispered. "He'll want to go to bed early, won't he?"

Was this the mistress equivalent of whistling in the dark?

She laid out several possible outfits for the evening, all the while knowing that she'd come here to be Kateb's mistress and that the spirit of their agreement insist she cooperate as best she could. Which meant wearing one of the traditional harem dresses left for her. After a few moments of indecision, not to mention a writhing stomach, she went into the dressing area to study the clothes.

They were all beautiful. Swirling diaphanous silk with exquisite stitching and beading. She picked up one done in tones of purple and dark green, then noticed a long cloak next to the dresses. It came to the floor and would cover her completely.

So no one else would see the prince's mistress, she thought, both horrified and relieved. She wouldn't have to parade half-naked in front of the palace staff. But wearing it seemed so…submissive. As if she'd agreed to all this.

Which she had.

She collected the dress and carried it to the bath. She

was about to sacrifice herself in the name of family honor. But before she did, she was going to have the best shower of her life and take a few laps in her new bathtub.

Victoria was ready on time. She'd put off the final stage of dressing until the last minute, then slipped the dress she'd chosen over her body. It was beautiful, whispering against her skin, cool and soft at the same time. As Yusra had promised, she wasn't as exposed as she'd feared. But her body was at least partially visible and she was naked underneath. Not exactly a style designed for peace of mind.

She just slipped on the cloak when a young woman appeared in the hallway, no doubt using the old servant's entrance. She nodded at Victoria.

"If you will come with me," she said.

Victoria followed her out the main door and through the palace. She saw dozens of rooms filled with low sofas and tables, three different dining rooms and a large library before being led into a maze of hallways that ended in front of a door as big as the one guarding the harem. Two guards stood on either side of it.

One of the men opened the door. The girl stepped back and motioned for Victoria to enter. She hesitated only a second before sucking in a breath and stepping over the threshold into Kateb's quarters.

She had a brief impression of space and light, beautiful sofas, a small table set for two and surrounded by cushions instead of chairs. There was a cart next to it with covered dishes. Dinner, she presumed, although she was too nervous to even think about eating.

Before she could figure out what she was supposed to do or where she was supposed to go, she saw Kateb walking toward her.

He wore loose white trousers and nothing else. His bare

chest, honey-colored and thick with muscles, gleamed in the lamplight. He had one towel around his shoulders and was using another to dry his hair. He didn't see her right away.

Her first reaction was that he almost looked like a regular guy—if one was in the habit of hanging out with underwear models. His loose-fitting clothes hadn't prepared her for his physical perfection. As views went, this was a nice one.

Her second reaction was that he didn't seem as intimidating or powerful. Maybe it was the towel, or the wet hair. But she found herself being slightly less afraid.

He dropped both towels onto a table, then ran his fingers through his hair, smoothing it into place. Only then did he see her.

One eyebrow raised. "Interesting outfit. Very Little Red Riding Hood."

She fingered the cloak. "I assume it's traditional to keep the harem girls protected. Apparently my status here is for your eyes only."

"So there's more?"

Was he teasing? Did he tease?

"A dress."

"Can I see it?"

Both nervous and afraid, she unfastened the tie at her neck and let the cloak fall to the floor.

Kateb's eyes widened slightly. His jaw clenched. Otherwise he didn't move, but she still wanted to cover herself. And maybe scream. As if the sharp sound could protect her.

"Yusra's doing?" he asked, turning away and walking to the table. A bottle of wine sat there. He poured two glasses, then shrugged into a shirt left draped across the pillows.

"It's not something I would buy," she snapped. "There are four more just like it. She told me that she wore something similar when she was young."

"I didn't need to know that," he muttered, then sipped the wine. He held out a glass to her, but she shook her head. "Are you hungry?"

Did he expect her to eat before he had his way with her? Or was she just supposed to stand there, practically naked and be the evening's entertainment? It was all she could do not to pull off one of her strappy gold sandals and throw it at him.

"Okay, look," she snapped. "This has gone on long enough. I'm tired, I'm jet-lagged or desert-lagged or whatever it is. I'm in a strange place and you're scaring me. What happens now? What does being your mistress mean? What are the ground rules? Daily sex? Weekly? Am I just supposed to assume the position whenever you say? And what kind of sex? Who's on top? What are you going to do to me?"

She had about a thousand more questions, but these seemed like enough for tonight. She folded her arms across her chest and did her best not to give in to the tears she could feel forming.

Kateb stared at her. "It is not my intention to frighten you."

"Then you're not doing a very good job."

"Apparently not." He picked up the second glass of wine and carried it over to her. "I have never had a mistress before, so I don't have any set expectations."

She took the wine without looking at him. "You have a harem."

"It came with the property."

"Sort of like a three-car garage when you only have two cars?"

"Something like that." He returned to the table and sank onto several of the cushions. "I am tired as well, Victoria. I will not seek your company in my bed tonight."

Another reprieve, she thought. But for how long? "What will you expect when you do?"

"There is more to being a mistress than simply sex. You are to provide me with companionship, to be entertaining."

"Like a trained bear?" She narrowed her gaze. "I don't know how to juggle, and if you're expecting one of the veil dances, you can forget it."

He sighed. "It is possible you're not true mistress material."

"You think?"

One corner of his mouth twitched. "Perhaps we will begin with you serving me dinner."

She stayed where she was. "Are we talking about me putting food on your plate or stuffing it directly into your mouth?"

"On my plate is sufficient."

"And no sex tonight. You swear?"

"You have my word as Prince Kateb of El Deharia."

She wanted to press for more, but giving his word was a big deal for the royal set. "We'll discuss the details later?"

"We will have full disclosure before anything happens."

"Which is not the same as agreeing to a talk after dinner."

"I know."

"You just want the last word," she grumbled as she approached the table. "It's just so typical."

She set her wineglass on the table and crossed to the cart. She removed the domed lids and found sliced roast, some kind of fancy potato dish she'd had at the palace and knew was delicious and made her hips spread just by looking at it, salad and vegetables.

She glanced over her shoulder. "Very Western. Do you always eat like this?"

"I enjoy a variety of food."

Did he enjoy a variety of women?

The question surprised her, although she didn't ask it. Maybe she didn't want to know. Under other circumstances she would have liked Kateb. Maybe too much.

She dished up the meal and passed him a plate, then took a much smaller serving for herself. She was still nervous enough that she wasn't sure how much she could eat.

Dining on cushions looked more romantic than it was, she thought as she tried to find a comfortable position. Kateb sprawled with a masculine grace that she found annoying, while she couldn't figure out how to sit comfortably in the stupid dress.

She managed to prop herself up and reached for her fork. "So you've never had a mistress, but have you had other women in the harem?"

"Not personally. Bahjat had about fifteen women." He smiled. "As they aged, he did not replace them. Perhaps out of affection or because it was not worth the effort. Regardless of the reason, by the time he was in his seventies, they were only a few years younger."

She laughed despite her tensions. "Geriatric harem girls? Seriously?"

"Yes. It could be startling when one came to dinner and was served by scantily clad women in their sixties."

"I can't even imagine." She speared a few green beans on her fork. "Will I be expected to serve at dinners?"

"No."

She nearly pointed out she'd already worked as a waitress so there wasn't a big difference. Then she remembered what she was doing here. Did she really want to serve a roomful of men wearing what she had on?

"So what are the rules as far as where I can go?" she asked. "Is the palace okay? The grounds? The village?

What am I supposed to do with my day? I'm used to working. Sex can only take so long. Six minutes. Eight, tops. That leaves a lot of free time."

Kateb looked at Victoria, who was blithely eating her dinner. "You insult me so freely?"

"What?" Her eyes widened and she looked genuinely confused. "Oh, you mean the time thing? I wasn't trying to be insulting."

"I'm sure the outcome will be impressive when you do."

She picked up her wine. "I'm sure it will take hours, but afterward, I still have a day to fill."

He found he enjoyed her company, when she forgot to be afraid. She reminded him a little of Cantara, who had known him most of her life. But with his late wife, there was always an element of separation. She was aware of him as the man in the relationship, of him as a prince. They would never be equals. Victoria had been raised in the West, where women and men were supposed to be more alike than they were different.

"You may go anywhere in the palace or the village. No one will bother you. But you are not to travel past the beginning of the fields."

"How will you know if I do?" she asked. "Will I be guarded? Have a collar with a bell?"

"If you leave the safety of the village, you will die," he said simply, knowing it to be true. "You will get lost and perish. That is your best hope. Otherwise you will be found by a raiding party. You would not enjoy their treatment."

She dropped her fork back to her plate and shivered. "Point taken," she murmured. "I've heard about raiding parties. Do they attack the village?"

"No. We are too many and too well protected, but they prey on those foolish enough to travel the desert on a whim. Or those who are too small to protect themselves."

Her gaze seemed drawn to his cheek. "I heard you were kidnapped when you were younger."

He nodded. "I was fifteen and out riding with my friends. They were lying in wait and took only me. The other boys returned here, but the raiders covered their tracks well. They demanded money from my father."

Millions, he thought, remembering how afraid he'd been. Not of the raiding party but of his father and Bahjat. He knew both men would be furious with him for being so foolish.

"Did the king pay?"

"I escaped before the negotiations could begin." *And killed a man in the process*, he thought grimly, not proud of his actions. But there had been no choice and taking that life had matured him well before his time. Word had traveled to the village, giving him a level of acceptance he hadn't experienced before. Even the king had been pleased by his bravery.

He hadn't ever told anyone taking a life wasn't brave.

"At least you got a scar out of it," she said. "You know that makes you a chick magnet."

"I do not need a scar."

"It helps."

She smiled as she spoke, making him aware of her mouth. He liked that she teased him, probably because no one else did.

When they finished dinner, she asked, "Am I expected to clear?"

"Of course."

"Next time I want to play the role of the handsome prince," she grumbled. "You can be the serving girl."

"Unlikely."

She rolled her eyes, then stood and reached for his plate. As she leaned toward him, the neckline of the dress gaped enough to allow him to see her breasts. They were perfectly formed and the right size for his hands. She straightened before he could look his fill, but the glimpse had been enough to show him that he would enjoy making love with her.

After putting the dirty plates on the tray, she hovered by the table. "Now what?"

"Coffee." He nodded at a folded screen in the corner.

She walked over and pulled it aside, then stood with her hands on her hips. "You have got to be kidding me." She stepped aside so he could see what he already knew was there.

"Yes?"

"What happened to being one with nature?" she demanded, then pointed at the espresso machine on the table. "You can foam milk with this. People who are one with the desert do not foam milk."

"Maybe it's goat's milk."

"Maybe you're just a metrosexual in disguise."

"You mock me?"

"Yes. This is me mocking you. An espresso machine? I can't believe it. You probably expect me to make you coffee."

"Of course."

"I hope it keeps you up tonight."

It wouldn't but she might, he thought, his gaze lingering on her waist and hips as she turned away and studied the machine.

"You're lucky," she said, picking up a pitcher of water and pouring it into the machine. "We have one just like this in the assistant's lunch room. I know what I'm doing."

He was more intriguing by the way she moved than the coffee she prepared. Her skin was pale, her legs long. She was beautiful, all curves and sass. Longing stirred and he knew it was for Victoria specifically rather than the itch of a biological need.

He had only ever wanted Cantara. What did it mean that

he desired Victoria? Was it because he knew her and he hadn't bothered to know any of the other women he'd been with? Was it proximity? Or was it her specifically?

He knew that behind the humor and the big blue eyes beat the heart of a mercenary. She had come to El Deharia to marry Nadim, knowing she would never love him. It had been about getting what she wanted. And yet…

"Foam?" she asked. "No foam?"

"No foam."

She set the cup on the table. "Anything else?"

He leaned back in the cushions and thought about her body next to his.

"You may kiss me."

The eyes he'd admired widened. "You promised." The words seemed forced out, against her will. She went pale.

He sensed her fear and reached for her hand. "I'll keep my promise," he told her, not sure why he felt compelled to reassure her. She was here to do his bidding, yet he didn't want her to be afraid. He squeezed her fingers. "A kiss isn't sex."

"So I've heard."

"One kiss." He pulled her down on the pillows.

She knelt next to him. "Is this the same as a guy saying 'Come up for coffee. Nothing will happen'?"

"I'm not a guy. I'm a prince."

"A technicality. Seriously, Kateb, I'm really not ready to…"

He raised his eyebrows.

She sighed. "One kiss."

"You might enjoy it."

"Maybe." She sounded doubtful.

She bent over him. Her long, curly blond hair tumbled down and lightly brushed his chest, making him wish he hadn't put on a shirt.

She braced herself on either side of his shoulders, leaned down and pressed her mouth to his.

At first there was nothing. Just a warm, skin-on-skin reaction that was pleasant, but not erotic. Then she moved slightly and he felt a jolt of fire burn through him. Need and hunger consumed him until he could only think that she must not stop kissing him.

Her lips were warm and soft and tempted him. She continued the kiss, pressing lightly, teasing. He reached for her, intending to pull her down next to him, only to remember his word.

One kiss.

He swore silently, wanting to feel her weight on him before he turned her, claiming her as his own. He burned and his arousal throbbed in time with his heartbeat.

She drew back and opened her eyes. Confusion swirled there, as did shock, making him confident she had felt the connection as well.

"Kateb?"

One kiss. He cursed himself for making the promise and giving his word. He could do nothing against such bonds, nothing but lie there, wanting what he could not have.

She touched her fingers to her mouth, then swallowed. "Maybe a second kiss wouldn't be such a bad thing."

Relief battled with desire. Released from his pledge, he pulled her down onto the pillows. "No, it would not."

Chapter Five

Victoria had been unable to stop herself. The second she'd touched Kateb's mouth with her own, she'd been swept away by a sensual wanting unlike anything she'd experienced before.

There had been men in her life—two—both of whom had been nice and sweet and eager to please her. She'd enjoyed the experience, had been comfortable making love. She'd felt anticipation, then pleasure, but never a driving need that made her mind go blank and her body tremble.

As Kateb pulled her against him, she went willingly, draping herself across him, body on body. If only they were skin on skin, she thought, as he turned her on the cushions and loomed over her. Then his mouth was on hers and she couldn't think about anything except how good it felt to have him take control.

He claimed her with a touch filled with yearning. Heat

poured through her. She wrapped her arms around his neck, both to touch him and to keep him close. He tilted his head, touching her lower lip with his tongue. She parted immediately, wanting to taste him and stroke him. Wanting him in her mouth, taking and giving.

He plunged inside, claiming her. He circled and danced. She did the same to him, each touch, each tingle making her more aware of maleness. Of him. Of all the possibilities.

He kissed her deeply, their breath mingling. The cushions yielded, then cradled her body. His hand moved up and down her back before sliding to her hip.

Although she was covered from shoulder to ankle, she was grateful the gossamer fabric didn't offer much of a barrier to his warm skin. If only he would touch her in other places. Her breasts, between her legs…she didn't want him to stop.

She touched his shoulders, his broad back, then his cool, silky hair. He broke the kiss, then pressed his mouth against her neck. She slipped her hands under his loose shirt to feel the delicious heat of his bare skin. He moved lower and, through the fabric took her right breast in his mouth.

The unexpected contact made her cry out in pleasure. Her nipples were hard and the wet gentle sucking drew up fire from the very center of her. Wanting was everywhere. Her bones were liquid, her very cells crying out for more and more and more.

It was a level of passion she'd never experienced before, a need that went so deep, she knew she would die if he didn't take her. She pulled frantically at his shirt. He sat up enough to remove it, then grabbed the front vee of her dress and ripped it in two.

The fabric gave instantly and she was naked before him. She shrugged out of the shredded material and reached for him.

"Not yet," he said, his voice low and thick with desire. "You are so perfect."

He looked at her, all of her, then touched her breasts with his finger. That single finger trailed down her belly. Down and down until her breath caught as she waited for what he would do to her.

No one had ever stared at her with such intensity, such possession. She should have been shy or worried about those extra fifteen pounds. Instead she watched him watch her and felt that place between her legs swell in anticipation.

At last he touched her there. A lone stroke that made her legs fall open and her breath catch. Then he was lowering himself to lick her belly before settling between her thighs with an intimate kiss that made her moan.

She was already trembling and close and desperate. He moved against her with a sureness that allowed her to relax into the experience even as tension tightened every muscle in her body. She clutched at pillows, dug her heels into the carpet and offered herself to him.

He cupped her hips, his fingers kneading her skin. His tongue moved against her in a steady rhythm she couldn't resist. Powerful tension and hunger burned until the trembling became shaking and her breath was only gasps.

Over and over he touched her, pushing her closer. She arched her head back and raced toward the moment when she would—

Her orgasm claimed her like a desert storm—fast and beautiful and out of control. She cried out as every part of her pulsed. He continued to move his tongue against her, easing her through her pleasure, drawing the last drop from her. When she was finally still, stunned by the power of her body's reaction to him, he quickly pulled off his trousers and plunged into her.

He was thick and hard and stretched her to perfection.

She wrapped her legs around him, pulling him in deeper, wanting to take all of him. She opened her eyes and found him watching her, his gaze intense. She couldn't look away. She could only watch the play of sexual tension across his face and know when he was getting close.

It was a level of intimacy completely unfamiliar to her, and even though it was frightening, she couldn't look away. Then he pushed in a little deeper and hit a spot that made her insides clench. An unexpected release claimed her again. She breathed his name. Her eyes closed. Seconds later, he groaned and was still.

Kateb wanted to tell himself he had taken Victoria unaware of who she was. That his need had been powerful and she had been conveniently naked. But through every stroke of their joining, he had known exactly who he was with and he had wanted *her* specifically. Now, still inside her slick heat, he stared into her blue eyes and didn't know what the hell he was supposed to say.

A case could be made that she had released him from his promise with her offer of a second kiss. Not much of a case, but it was the best he could do. Claiming he had been overwhelmed was true, but not something he would admit.

She appealed to him on a physical level. Not a bad quality in a mistress. Except he'd never thought to truly claim her as his. He'd brought her to the Winter Palace because she had offered herself in exchange for her father. Perhaps he'd brought her to punish her, although he couldn't name her crime.

He withdrew. Reluctantly.

She scrambled to her feet, nearly kicking him in her haste. She grabbed the pieces of her dress and held them up to her body.

"So you really hate the dress," she murmured before stepping off the cushions and picking up her cloak. In seconds, she was covered.

"Am I allowed to just go?" she asked, not looking at him. "Or do I have to ask for permission?"

"You may leave."

She nodded once and was gone.

He rose more slowly and pulled on his trousers. She'd left the dress, which he picked up and squeezed in his hands.

This wasn't supposed to happen. Not like this. Yes, she'd been obviously willing during their lovemaking, but that didn't erase his responsibility. Still, apologizing was not his way. He was a prince.

He told himself she'd enjoyed the experience. That he had pleased her. She'd responded to his touch, had been wet and swollen when he'd entered her, yet he couldn't push away the thought that he'd taken her against her will.

"That did not happen," he said aloud. "She was willing in every way."

Very willing. Too willing?

Had he played into her hands? Was the fear nothing more than an act? Had she hoped this would happen, thinking she could shame him into marriage? Was he her next Nadim? She wanted to marry a prince. Had she planned everything with her father? Was he a fool to worry about her?

Two extreme points of view, he thought grimly. Which was true? Or did the truth lie somewhere in the middle?

He walked into his bedroom. Despite his recent release, thinking about what had just happened made him want her again. He could call her back, insist she submit to him. But he would not.

Victoria was a complication he didn't need. A distraction. *Women*, he thought, feeling tired. With Cantara things had been easy, as they were with the other women he saw occasionally. There was no confusion—just an understanding of the expectations. That he was there for the night and nothing more.

What did Victoria expect and did he care? Was she truly sacrificing herself or playing a game? How was he to find the truth?

Victoria spent a restless night and woke feeling tired. She showered in the amazing bathroom, but didn't feel as at home as she had the night before. The beautiful space seemed to mock her a little, which was insane. Hadn't she fulfilled her mistress destiny by sleeping with Kateb? Didn't that make her one of the girls?

Nothing made sense, she thought as she dressed in a short-sleeved T-shirt and long skirt. On the one hand, she couldn't really regret what she'd done. Kateb had dazzled pretty much every cell in her body and who wouldn't want that in a lover? She was here for six months—wasn't enjoying him in bed better than the alternative?

On the other hand, she was a little freaked out by being so incredibly swept away. That had never happened to her before. She'd never felt such desperate need or so out of control. It felt as if she'd given him a part of herself and she couldn't get it back.

"Deep, deep thoughts," she murmured, and she only knew one way to restore her equilibrium.

Shopping.

She tucked some El Deharian currency into her pocket, found her sunglasses and tested Kateb's statement that she could come and go as she pleased, as long as she didn't head out of the village.

No one stood at the door of the harem when she left. She paused in the long corridor, not sure which way to turn.

She picked a direction and started walking. The main part of the castle was basically a square. If she kept on going, eventually she would run into the front foyer.

She saw dozens of people, some in traditional clothing, others in Western suits and dresses. A few smiled at her, most ignored her, but no one asked her what she was doing. After a few minutes, she recognized some of the art on the walls and figured she was heading in the right direction. Five minutes later, she found herself in the massive foyer and from there it was an easy walk to the bazaar.

The open stores and carts reminded her of the markets in the main city. She smiled at vendors, admired a few shawls, then turned a corner and stopped in front of an amazing display of woven gold.

Each piece was exquisite, delicate and gleaming in the sun. There were bracelets and necklaces, earrings in the shapes of flowers and hearts.

"Very pretty," the woman behind the counter said in English. "You like?"

"It's all lovely. I've never seen a selection this big before. Is it made locally?"

"Yes. Here in the village. You are from the city?"

Victoria nodded. She hadn't brought enough money to buy anything, which was really too bad. Or maybe not. The temptation to put a sizeable chunk on her credit card would be hard to resist.

"Who makes the jewelry?" she asked.

"Three or four families. The women work together. Mother to daughter, as it has been for many years."

The skills passed on to each generation? No wonder the work was so perfect. "Is it close? Could I see where they make the jewelry?"

The other woman nodded slowly. "Yes, you come. This afternoon." She gave her directions.

Victoria smiled. "I look forward to it. Thank you."

"You are welcome." She hesitated. "You are with Kateb?"

Victoria tried not to blush. "Yes. I'm with Kateb." Whatever that meant.

"He is a good man. He will be nominated as leader. We all miss Bahjat. Kateb is very lonely these days. Perhaps with you here…" Her voice trailed off.

Victoria frowned. Yusra had also mentioned Kateb being lonely. What was up with that? The man had a harem he could fill with as many women as he wanted. How lonely could he be?

Yusra arrived in Kateb's office fifteen minutes after he'd sent for her. She bowed slightly.

"It is good to have you back in the Winter Palace," she said.

"It will always be my home." He motioned her to sit, then abruptly rose and paced to the window. It had taken only a few hours for him to come to the obvious solution to his problem. "Victoria must return to the city. You will pack up her things and arrange transportation. She is to be gone before noon tomorrow."

He stared out at the courtyard as he spoke. Dozens of people came and went, looking busy and determined. He was just like them, with responsibilities. He didn't have time for a woman's plan to trap him.

"I am surprised," Yusra said slowly. "She displeased you so quickly?"

Victoria hadn't displeased him, which was part of the problem. He'd felt…unsettled after their encounter. A strange state of being he did not want to repeat. Having her gone was the best solution. She would attempt to find a different rich husband, trick another man. He would not fall prey to her.

"She is fine," he said, still not looking at Yusra. "But I

have no time for her. With the elders about to meet, I must deal with my responsibilities."

"She is one woman, Prince Kateb. How much trouble could she be?"

"You have no idea. My mind is made up. I want her gone."

"As you wish, sir."

He heard the older woman stand. He looked back at her, prepared to wish her good day. She spoke first.

"And if she is with child?"

Six simple words that changed everything, he thought grimly. Pregnant. He hadn't considered the possibility. Last night he'd be unable to think of anything but having her.

He didn't bother to question how Yusra knew they'd had sex. The ripped dress would have been clue enough and he'd left it on a chair in his rooms. Word would have spread quickly. He knew there were those who wanted him to take another wife, to have a child. They would hope Victoria was someone he would consider.

Or at least they would unless they found out the truth about her.

Could she be pregnant?

He hadn't thought to use protection. Was she on birth control? He remembered her plan to marry Nadim. No doubt had he been willing to take her to his bed, she would have been delighted to use pregnancy to trap him. There was no reason to assume she would act any differently with him.

He returned his gaze to Yusra. "She can't be allowed to leave until we know if she is pregnant or not."

"As you wish."

"You will tell me either way?"

"Of course. In no more than twenty-eight days, sir. Then you can let her go."

Having her gone tomorrow would be easier, but not possible. A little less than a month. That shouldn't be a problem. As Yusra had pointed out, Victoria was only one woman. He could handle her easily.

Exactly at three, Victoria knocked on the door of the old house on the corner. A woman answered right away. She was probably close to fifty, tall and very beautiful, with dark hair hanging in a long ponytail and large, expressive eyes. Gold chains hung around her neck and bangles jingled on both wrists.

"You must be Victoria," she said warmly. "Welcome. I am Rasha."

"Thank you so much for letting me see where you work," Victoria said as she stepped into the building.

From the outside it looked like a house, but on the inside, it was a big, open space with skylights and windows. The floors were stone. Interior walls had been removed and work stations set up in several places. Heat billowed from the left side, where several women poured molten gold into molds.

"I've admired your jewelry ever since I came to El Deharia two years ago," Victoria said. "I just didn't know it was yours. I bought these in the market in the city."

Rasha touched her earrings. "Yes, I recognize the piece. Very nice."

"They're beautiful. The weaving is incredible."

Rasha led her around the room. "We use many techniques to make our jewelry. Molds, as you see them doing here. The weaving involves long wires or threads that are just soft enough to bend. The delicate beadwork is the most difficult. We also set stones."

Rasha introduced her to many of the women working in the house, then showed her their inventory. The rows of completed work was dazzling and for a moment Victoria felt a little light-headed.

"I'm practically a professional shopper," she joked. "Seeing this much all in one place isn't good for me."

Rasha laughed. "We get used to it."

"That's almost sad." Victoria touched a pendant. "I know you sell in the city and here in the village. Anywhere else?"

"We have a man who takes our jewelry to El Bahar and Bahania. They do well."

Both neighboring countries, Victoria thought. But still relatively small markets.

"What about selling on the Internet?"

Rasha frowned. "Is that possible?"

"Sure. You set up a Web site with pictures and set prices. You'd have to deal with shipping and boxes and insurance. I wonder if mailing into other countries would be a problem? Customs and import fees. Maybe it would be better to find a distributor in, say, the U.S. and Europe."

"You have many ideas," Rasha told her. "We are a small factory. No one would be interested in what we have to offer."

"Don't underestimate your work. People would be very interested. Handmade jewelry is something to treasure. Your prices are reasonable and the work itself is exquisite. I think you could be very successful."

Several of the women had stopped working to listen. Victoria couldn't tell if they were interested or if they were shocked she'd disagreed with Rasha.

"It would be nice not to be dependent on the only person who takes our things to El Bahara and Bahania," Rasha said slowly. "He does not always give us a good price."

A few of the women nodded.

"I don't want to push," Victoria said, excited about the idea of helping these women be more successful. Still, this was a different culture. Change came slowly. "Would you mind if I talked to Kateb about what I've seen and a few of my ideas? If he approved…"

Rasha's eyes lit up. "You would speak to the prince on our behalf?"

"Of course. I know he's concerned about growing the economy here. Selling your jewelry abroad would bring in a lot of money. If nothing else, maybe I could set up a Web site for you and see if there's any interest."

She wondered how products found their way to the home shopping channels on American TV. Something she would have to look into.

Rasha glanced around the room. All the women had stopped working and were listening.

"Please," she said, smiling at Victoria. "If the prince thinks this is a good idea, we would appreciate any help you could give us."

"I'll talk to him as soon as I can, then get some ideas together." She ignored the slight flutter in her stomach at the thought of seeing Kateb again. It wasn't as if she was looking forward to another evening with him.

Not that it was a good sign when she started lying to herself, she thought glumly. She *was* looking forward to seeing him and was just twisted enough to be thrilled to have an excuse.

Which meant what? That she'd enjoyed the sex? Silly question, of course she had. Or did this mean something more? That she actually liked the man?

Alarm bells went off in her head. Liking was the first step in the slick road to feeling more and she knew the danger of that.

She shook off the thoughts. "I'll be back in a few days to tell you what he said."

"Thank you." Rasha picked up a bracelet and handed it to her. "In honor of your visit."

The bracelet was beautiful—links of gold that seemed to glow.

"While I'm seriously tempted, I'm going to say no. It's too much. Save it. If I can help, then I'll accept it gladly."

Rasha hesitated, then nodded. "I look forward to seeing you again."

"Me, too."

They walked to the front of the house. Rasha let her out. Victoria noticed a young boy playing in the garden.

"Sa'id," Rasha said sharply. "Do not stop here. Go at once."

The boy looked up. He was thin and shabbily dressed, but when he saw Victoria, he smiled.

"Your hair is very pretty," he said. "I haven't seen anything like it."

She smiled back and said, "Thank you," when what she was really thinking was where on earth would she get highlights done in the middle of the desert? She waved at Rasha and at the boy, then hurried in the direction of the Winter Palace.

She should see Kateb right away, she told herself. If only to talk to him about the women and her plans to take them global. She thought about how he'd kissed her the previous night and the feel of his hands on her body and found herself not-so-secretly hoping he planned to have his way with her again.

Soon.

Chapter Six

Victoria returned to the harem to change her clothes before going to see Kateb. She told herself it was because she wanted to be professional when she talked to him about Rasha and the women making jewelry, but she didn't actually believe the words.

She kept on the long skirt, but replaced comfortable sandals she could walk in with a high-heeled pair. She exchanged her T-shirt for a fitted camisole-style blouse with lace, added an ankle bracelet, freshened her makeup, then had to press her hand to her stomach to quell the sudden attack of anxious butterflies.

"This is no big deal," she whispered to herself. "It's just Kateb."

Whom she had recently seen naked and made love with.

She was both excited and nervous, while oddly uncomfortable. Not a combination of emotions designed to put her into a meditative state, she thought, trying to find humor because it was better than fear or worry.

She left the harem and went in search of the offices. All working palaces had offices where the day-to-day details were handled. Government required files and computers and good lighting. Even in a thousand-year-old palace.

As she explored, she told herself that she'd traveled with Kateb to be his mistress, but the concept wasn't real to her. It was a scene in a book or a movie—not her life. No wonder she was still finding her way. Yet last night it had been very real, complete with incredible sex with a sheik she barely knew. If she'd been asked before they'd been intimate, she would have sworn she wasn't capable of being swept away so completely. Now she knew differently.

But was it the circumstances or the man? Which was better? That she'd given in to passion because it had been a long time and the guy knew what he was doing? Or was it specifically about him? Was there something else? Something more powerful and frightening?

She didn't want it to be the latter. If it was, she was in danger. She could be hurt or worse. Look at her mother. No—she wasn't attracted to Kateb in a relationship kind of way. Her heart was firmly locked away and nothing was going to change that.

Which left chemistry. Fine. They were good together in bed. She hadn't experienced that sort of attraction before but as long as she didn't make it more than it was, she would be fine. Think of the calories she could burn in a night with him.

She made her way to the rear of the palace, then followed a couple of guys in Western dress up to the second floor. Stone walls gave way to sensible drywall and offices. She walked toward a serious man in a suit, sitting behind a large desk.

"I'd like to see Kateb," she told him.

The man was probably a couple of years younger than her. He was the equivalent of a receptionist, but she could tell by the way he looked at her that he thought he was just a little better than everyone else.

"The prince is busy." His tone of voice dismissed her.

"How do you know I don't have an appointment?"

"Because I manage his calendar."

She doubted that. Kateb would have a personal assistant who took care of the details. Desk Boy would probably have a copy on his computer, nothing more.

"You might want to tell him I'm here," she said, smiling pleasantly.

Desk Boy looked her up and down. "I don't think so," he said. "Now if you'll excuse me."

He turned back to his computer.

Victoria wanted to slap him. Instead she gave him an even bigger smile. "The blonde thing should be a clue. Do you see many Americans out here? I'm guessing you don't. You should also listen better when you're getting your coffee, because I'm going to guess that there's been plenty of chatter about Kateb's new mistress. That would be me. Now you can take me to him or I can find my way there myself and complain about you. Either works. Which is it going to be?"

"I know who you are," Desk Boy said with a sneer. "I know exactly who and what you are. Go away."

Victoria took a step back. She felt as if she'd been slapped. Culturally, mistresses were slightly below the queen but above everyone else. It was considered respectable, even an honor, to be the prince's mistress. While she'd had personal issues about sleeping with Kateb, she'd never worried about how she would be treated by his people.

She didn't know what to do or say. Before she could

come up with a plan, she sensed someone coming up behind her. A heartbeat later, she felt a warm hand on the small of her back as Kateb moved next to her.

"She is mine," he said, his voice low and cold. "And therefore an extension of me."

Desk Boy went pale and stood. "Yes, S-Sir," he stammered. He turned to Victoria. "My apologies."

Too little, too late, she thought but didn't say. Instead she nodded and relaxed a little as the heat from Kateb's hand warmed her.

He guided her down the long corridor, then into a huge office. Once he took his hand away, she felt herself start to shake.

"He was so rude," she whispered. "I didn't expect that. The look on his face…"

"It's not about you," he told her, closing the door. "He comes from a powerful family. His eldest brother died a few years ago. He was a good man and well liked. The family believes if he had lived, he would have been chosen by the elders as the next leader."

"Is that true?"

"Who is to say? Probably not. Last year his father approached me, trying to arrange a marriage between me and the family's oldest daughter. I refused."

That could be awkward, she thought. "So basically the family hates you."

"No. The daughter was in love with someone else and grateful I refused her."

"Was that the reason you did?"

He shrugged. "We would not have suited each other."

She doubted that was the real reason. Kateb had been nice and he would hate anyone to know about it. "So it's just Desk Boy who has the attitude?"

"Desk Boy?"

"You know who I mean."

"I will send him to the city. Some time working for one of my brothers will distract him."

Victoria wouldn't be sorry to see him go. "Now that we've solved that problem, I need to talk to you about something."

He walked around to his desk and sat down. "Which is?"

There was something about the way he looked at her, she thought, unable to figure out what he was thinking. Almost as if he were angry with her. Yet he'd rescued her. Or had that been about claiming what was his? About his station rather than hers?

"Victoria?" He sounded impatient.

She approached the desk. It was large and carved. The room itself had to be at the base of one of the towers—the window walls angled, forming a rough semicircle. There were rugs and low sofas and an air of importance that reminded her of King Mukhtar's office in the city.

"I went to the bazaar today," she began. "There is a small store selling locally made jewelry. I've seen it before and bought some." She fingered her earrings. "The work is beautiful. Original and contemporary but with enough traditional elements to make each piece timeless."

He leaned back in his chair and looked bored. "And?"

"They only sell here and in the city. Some guy takes their stuff to El Bahar and Bahania, but I think he might be ripping them off. Rasha didn't sound that thrilled with him." She drew in a deep breath. "I think they could do more. I think they could sell all over the world and be really successful. I don't want to get too ahead of myself, but we could start with a Web site. I could even put it together. I'm not great at them, but I've taken a few classes and I'm sure I could help. I don't know about selling to other countries, though. We'd probably need some kind of distribution arrangement or customs would be a nightmare. Maybe a catalog, too. And I don't know about the money. There are those services that collect it for you. That would be good."

She paused for breath and because Kateb was staring past her, as if he wasn't listening.

Then his gaze swung back to her, only it wasn't the least bit friendly. She felt the chill down to her ankle bracelet.

"Are you on birth control?" he asked.

"What?"

He waited, practically glaring at her. "Are you?"

Birth control. As in…

Her mouth dropped open. She consciously closed it. Because they'd had sex. He hadn't used a condom, which meant the whole protection element was up to her.

Technically she was supposed to wait to be invited to sit, but suddenly that didn't seem so very important. She sank into one of the chairs in front of the desk.

"I never thought…" she began.

"You're not." It wasn't a question.

"No."

"Because you wished to trap Nadim. Had you tried to get him into your bed? Did you hope to get pregnant, forcing him to marry you?"

She sprang to her feet. "What? Are you crazy? I would never do that."

"And I should take your word on that?"

"He was my *boss*. I was completely respectful of him and his position the entire time we worked together."

"You wanted to marry him."

Was he being difficult on purpose? "I already explained that. It wasn't about him, it was about feeling safe. About not having to worry about what would happen the next time my father showed up. You met him. He offered me in a card game. How would that make you feel?"

"So if not Nadim, then any rich man would do? You must be very pleased with our deal. Did you plan the whole thing with your father? Did he cheat on purpose?"

If he'd been closer, she would have slapped him. A serious mistake that could land her in jail, but right now she didn't care.

"How dare you?" she demanded. "I told you the truth. You were there when it happened. You may have only known my father a few hours, but I am confident you recognized the type. I'm not like him. I gave my word to you because I'd given it to my dying mother. There's no other reason."

She was so angry she wanted to throw something, or cry. But she stood there, not doing either, not giving in to the emotions pouring through her.

He rose and walked toward her. "You will not win this, Victoria. I am clear on who and what you are and I will never trust you. You chose to play the game and you lost. You will never win me."

"I'm not interested in winning you," she yelled. "Talk about an ego."

"When this is done, you will gain your freedom, nothing more."

"I don't want anything else." She never wanted to see him again. "Do you think I planned all this? Do you think I walked around hoping you would lose control last night and then sleep with me?"

"It was your ultimate plan."

"You're wrong. I would never do that."

"I don't believe you."

"You're the one who broke his word," she snapped. "Nothing was supposed to happen. Do you remember that? You promised."

Something flashed across his face. "You released me from my word."

"Oh, sure. That's a very typical male response. Don't bother taking responsibility. *You* chose to have sex with me, Kateb. *You* didn't bother using a condom. This is just as much your fault. But we're not going to talk about that, are we? No, let's just blame the woman. That's so much easier than the truth."

She put her hands on her hips, her anger giving her strength. "And while we're on the subject of unprotected sex, should I be worried? Did one of your other chickies leave you a nasty gift?"

His gaze narrowed. "You dare question me?"

"Someone has to."

"There is no reason for concern." He seemed to speak between clenched teeth.

"Good to know. So here's my question—you brought me here to be your mistress. Maybe it's just me, but isn't sex implied in the position? Oh, wait. You thought so, too. You told me in the desert that I wouldn't be in your bed until we got here. So when exactly did you plan to have the birth-control conversation with me? You're so smart and princelike. Why would you assume? If your damn sperm are so precious, you should protect them from scheming women willing to trick you into bed."

He stiffened, then seemed to grow taller. He opened his mouth, but before he could speak, she interrupted him.

"Don't even bother with the whole 'I'm Prince Kateb' blah, blah, blah. I'm not the bad guy here. I didn't do anything wrong. You never asked if I was on birth control. You should have found out before we did it."

"Return to the harem," he growled.

"So it's a prison now? I won't be allowed out? Are you breaking your word on that, too?" She was shaking, both from fury and fear. He was a powerful man and they were in the middle of the desert. If she disappeared, who would know? Who would bother to come looking for her?

But she couldn't let the fear win. She'd learned that a long time ago. She had to be strong, to stand up for herself. No one else was going to do it.

"Return to the harem," he repeated. "You will stay here, in the village, until I know if you are pregnant or not."

She didn't like the sound of that. "If I'm not?"

"You will be returned to the city."

She didn't bother asking what would happen if she was. She knew enough of El Deharian law to know a royal child would never be allowed to be taken away. That if she wanted any contact with her child, she would be trapped here forever.

There was so much she wanted to say, so much he didn't understand. But what was the point? He'd made up his mind about her long before he met her. Nothing would change it now.

She turned and left.

Victoria almost wasn't surprised to find Yusra in the harem.

"Do you know about this?" she asked the other woman. "Did he tell you?"

The older woman's expression remained calm. "Kateb is concerned."

"He's a jackass," Victoria muttered. "I wish I'd thought to tell him that. He blames me. Did he mention that? It's all my fault, because I tricked him. Oh, yeah, my whole plan finally worked out." She sank onto one of the cushioned sofas and covered her face with her hands. "I didn't do this on purpose. Why can't he see that?"

Yusra sat next to her. "He will. In time."

"Want to bet?"

What was worse than all the things he said was how dirty she felt inside. As if she'd done something wrong.

"Kateb isn't like other men," Yusra told her.

"He's just as stupid as they are."

"That is true," the other woman said, then smiled when Victoria looked at her. "Men see what they want to see."

"He thinks I'm only after what I can get. That I'm tricking him."

"For now. He will calm down and see reason."

"Want to give me a date when that's going to happen?"

"Soon."

"Now you're just saying things to make me feel better." Victoria dropped her hands to her lap and sagged back against the sofa.

"Come with me," Yusra said as she stood.

Victoria hesitated. "You're not taking me to the dungeon, are you?"

"No. There is something you should see."

Yusra stood, waiting patiently until Victoria stood and followed her. They walked down several hallways before walking into a large room that was totally empty. There were big windows, but no furniture. Before she could ask the point of their visit, she turned and saw a massive tapestry on the wall.

It was perhaps twenty square feet and had to have taken dozens of women several generations to complete it.

Victoria approached it slowly, taking in the detail of the huge family tree. Up close she could see the tiny stitches, the intricate and perfect work.

"This is Kateb," Yusra said simply. "He can trace his family back over a thousand years. Their blood has been spilled on the sand, their sons and daughters have lived and died here. To be one with the royal family is to have a place in history."

Victoria had grown up in a small Texas town where she'd hated that everyone knew her past. That everyone knew her father was useless and a gambler and that they were poor. She'd wanted to go somewhere else and start over, without that horrible legacy following her everywhere.

But this was different, she thought, wishing she could touch the tapestry but knowing better. This was living history. This wasn't about one generation or one king. This was about a dynasty that had survived longer than many governments.

A stab of longing cut through her. Not to be royal but to be a part of something bigger than herself. Something more important.

"If you have his child, your name will be added," Yusra told her.

"That's a big *if*. And if I have his child, I'm trapped here forever."

"Life is not a trap."

"Sometimes it feels like it." Like now.

A baby? She didn't think it was possible.

She considered Kateb's words—that she would have trapped Nadim with a pregnancy. Honestly, she couldn't imagine going on a date with him, let alone sleeping with him. No, Nadim had represented a kind of security she'd never experienced. Nothing more. Not that she would ever convince Kateb of that.

If she was pregnant, everything would change. Did she want that? Her name on the tapestry? A child with Kateb?

The answer came quickly. No. Not like this. Not with him believing she'd tricked him. Not with them angry and accusing each other. That was no way to bring a child into the world.

"If I'm not pregnant, he said I could go," she told Yusra. "Is that what you want?"

She thought about how he had been the previous night. The passion that had consumed them. She thought about the man who had brought her electricity for her curling iron, despite the fact that they were in the desert.

There was kindness there—perhaps a good and gentle man. But she wasn't interested in giving her heart and he would never see her as anything but a woman out for what she could get.

"Yes," Victoria said. "I want to leave. I guess it will take a couple of weeks to know if that's going to happen."

Yusra stared at her. "You would go so easily?"

"I've barely known Kateb a week."

"Still, he is the prince."

"You sound disappointed."

"I am. Kateb must marry soon. If he does not pick a bride, one will be found for him."

An arranged marriage? "I wouldn't think he would allow that," she said. "He's too stubborn to let someone else influence his life that way."

"Yet he will let it happen." Yusra looked as if she had more to say, but she was silent.

"I'll believe that when I see it."

"No, you will not. You will be gone."

She was right, something that should have made Victoria happy. But it didn't. Talk about trapped, she thought sadly. She didn't want to stay and maybe, just maybe, she didn't want to go. Which left her nowhere.

Kateb found himself so distracted during his late-afternoon meetings that he had to reschedule them for the next day so the points in question could be addressed. He resented his inability to focus on the concerns of the elders and knew there was only one cause.

Victoria.

Tomorrow would be better, he told himself as he made his way back to his rooms, only to find the cause of his inattention waiting for him there.

Victoria sat on a sofa, reading a fashion magazine. She hadn't heard him approach, so she didn't look up. He was able to study her without being observed.

Her long, curly blond hair tumbled down her shoulders. The soft gold color made his fingers ache to feel the silkiness. Her lush curves threatened to spill from the sleeveless top she wore and the long, layered skirt seem to call to him to explore what was hidden.

How could he want her? Knowing what he did, he should resent her, or at least not think of her. But she had haunted him all day. Even through his anger, he wanted her and that offended him most of all.

He must have made a sound because she looked up, then dropped the magazine onto the cushion before standing.

"They're saying navy is going to be big this fall," she told him. "It's the new black. Have you noticed they're always saying this or that color is the new black? There actually isn't a new black, no matter what they want us to believe. There's just the old black." She paused, then sighed. "You have no idea what I'm talking about, nor do you care."

His voice was rough. "Why are you here?"

"To talk to you about Rasha and the other women making jewelry. We were so busy with your overwrought accusations that we never got to talk about that."

For some reason, he couldn't seem to summon the anger. It should have been there—she had earned it—yet it was nowhere to be found.

"I am not overwrought," he told her sternly.

"Want to take a vote on that?" She held up her hands. "Never mind. I'll stay on topic. The women should be selling in places other than the city marketplace and to the camel guy."

"That is their decision, not mine."

"Au contraire, great prince. You're the man, or at least you will be when the elders pick you. Everyone knows it's going to happen, so they're acting as if it already has. Rasha got all quivery when I mentioned talking to you about them selling elsewhere. They need your permission. And as I don't have a computer of my own to get started on this…I do, too."

She didn't sound happy about the fact.

"You are very persistent."

"Someone has to be. They deserve a chance at this. A chance to make a living." Her blue eyes flashed with annoyance. "And while we're on the subject of making a living, I'm going to need access to my savings account while I'm here."

"Why?"

"To buy things."

"Whatever you want will be provided."

"Does a little man with a bucket of gold follow me everywhere I go? What if I want to go into the bazaar and buy a dress or something?"

"They'll bill me."

"I don't think so." She glared at him. "I have money, I just need access to it."

"While you are here, you are my responsibility."

"Not really. I'm just the money-hungry tramp who tricked you into sleeping with her. Isn't that the story you're telling yourself?"

He crossed to the armoire in the corner, opened the doors and poured himself a drink. "You want anything?" he asked, before picking up his glass.

"No, thank you."

He swallowed the scotch, knowing it wasn't nearly enough to help. He turned back to her.

"It wasn't what you think," she said. "Nadim was very much more a theory than a man. I didn't want to be that little girl in the charity clothes. I didn't want to have to stand in line to get a special meal. I don't expect you to believe me, but it's the truth."

She spoke defiantly, as if she *did* expect him to believe her but knew he would never take the time.

What was the truth? It would be relatively easy to investigate her past and determine what had actually happened. And as soon as he had the thought, he realized he did believe her. At least about that.

"I was going back to the States," she continued. "I was going to figure out what to do with my life and open my own business. You can ask Maggie. That's Qadir's fiancée."

"I know who Maggie is."

"She's my friend. She knows what I was thinking."

"Nadim would not have made you happy."

"You mean because he's lacking a personality?"

He did his best not to laugh. "That is part of the problem."

"Let me guess. The other part is he's male. Your gender has some real issues."

He stared at her. "Must I remind you who I am?"

"No, but I have a feeling you will anyway." She shook her head. "I didn't try to trick either of you. I didn't even want to fall in love. I saw what it did to my mom. Love is for suckers."

He sensed she believed the words. "You're too young to be so cynical."

"And yet, here I stand." She moved toward him. "Kateb, I'm not pregnant. It was one time and the odds are seriously against it. At the risk of providing you with too much information, I just finished my period last week. That makes it even more unlikely. I understand you want to be sure. So do I. But I'm not playing you. I never was."

Her blue eyes promised she spoke the truth and he found himself wanting to accept her words.

"We will see," he said instead.

Victoria sighed. "I guess so. So now let's talk about Rasha and the jewelry. This would be good thing for the village. Weren't you talking about diversification? Plus, the women need a little power."

"How do you know?"

"It's El Deharia. Sure, the country is very forward-thinking, but come on. Are you saying they get an equal vote at home?"

"Probably not."

Her suggestion had merit and he would be a fool to ignore it simply because of the source.

"Bring me a business plan," he said. "I will consider it."

She grinned, which made him want to kiss her—which annoyed him.

"Great. I even know how to write one. There wouldn't happen to be a spare computer anywhere?"

"I will have one delivered to your rooms. Anything else?"

"M&M's? Any color. I'm not fussy."

"You want candy?"

"I want chocolate. There's a difference."

He sighed. "You may go now."

She turned and left.

He found himself watching her walk across the room. His gaze dropped to her ridiculous high-heeled sandals. They were impractical and foolish and they suited her perfectly.

For a moment he wondered if the same held true for her? That she suited *him* perfectly.

Chapter Seven

Kateb heard the loud clacking sound in the hallway and knew that Victoria approached. He hadn't seen her in several days, which was to his liking. The less contact they had, the better. Unfortunately not seeing her had not removed her from his mind. He couldn't seem to go an hour without images of her haunting him. Memories of her naked body filled his dreams at night causing him to awaken hard, hungry and restless.

He heard voices outside his office, then the door opened and she strolled in. He looked at her and raised his eyebrows.

"I know, I know," she said, rolling her eyes. "Yusra brought it to me. Apparently it's traditional and as I'm your mistress, I'm the one stuck wearing it. I had a hard time finding the right shoes and I don't know what to do with my hair. What goes with the 'Hey, look, I'm the local harem girl'? I was thinking of just leaving it loose. Your thoughts?"

He took in the two-piece outfit that was more costume than clothing. The top was part bikini, part short vest, done in quilted silk and heavy beading. Her midsection was bare, and the silky trousers sat low on her hips. There was more beading in front and at the bands that hugged her ankles. Everywhere else, the fabric was sheer.

"Yusra has a sense of humor," he murmured, knowing the old woman wasn't the least bit subtle. She wanted him to consider Victoria as more than a temporary fixture in the palace.

"You think?" Victoria turned so he could see the sheer fabric in back, making her rear completely visible. "I'm not comfortable with the whole world seeing my butt."

She was close enough to naked that his body reacted predictably. He tried telling himself it was because he hadn't been with a woman in so long. Except he had…just last week. And the wanting wasn't about biological need— it was about being with Victoria again. Touching her and tasting her. Pleasing her and being pleased.

He moved behind his desk so his condition was not obvious.

"How did you get here?" he asked. "Or is palace staff different than the entire village?"

"I have a cloak. Desert fashion seems very cloak oriented. This one is beautiful. The beading matches. Shoes were a problem." She held out a foot, showing him her high-heeled sandals.

He glanced at them, then wished he hadn't when his gaze traveled up her bent leg to her thigh. He quickly looked at the report on his desk.

"You are not expected to wear that to the nominating ceremony," he said, thinking no one would pay attention to the elders if she did. "Regular clothes are fine. In fact you don't have to attend at all."

"I thought it might be interesting. I've never been to one. But if you don't want me there, that's fine. I heard the camel is in and I'm hoping he brought my new issue of *People* magazine."

There was something about the way she spoke, as if she were protecting herself from something. "Do you want to attend?" he asked.

She shrugged.

"Victoria?"

She sighed. "Look, I'm lonely, okay? No one talks to me but you and Yusra. I know Rasha and she's really nice, but she has a job. I'm working on the business plan, which is harder to do in real life than in a college class, and I'm making great progress, but that only fills eight or ten hours a day. I have nothing to do. Everything is done for me. It's boring."

"I thought you wanted a life of leisure."

"Do *not* go there again," she said, and put her hands on her hips.

The action wasn't the least bit intimidating. Not only because she was more kitten than tiger, but because it would be difficult to take anyone seriously in that costume.

"I wanted security, not days of lying around eating bonbons. I've worked my whole life. I'm used to doing things. Seeing people. I need to be useful."

She raised her chin as she spoke, as if daring him to dismiss her words.

"What would you like to do?" he asked instead.

"Well, it depends. Assuming I'm not pregnant, I'll be gone in a couple of weeks. Getting the proposal together for Rasha should be enough. But if I have to stay here longer, I was thinking about maybe trying to catalogue the art in the palace. There are plenty of books in the library to help and we could call in an expert if I got stuck."

She continued to surprise him. Perhaps a case could be

made that was a good thing. "We will discuss it when the time comes," he told her. "Now if you wish to attend the ceremony, you will need to change."

She glanced down at herself and smiled. "Only if you're sure."

He would prefer her in nothing, but that wasn't possible. He'd vowed he would not take her again. But right now, the reasons for that promise didn't seem at all clear.

"Go change," he told her. "You have an hour. If you are late…"

She'd already started for the door. "I know, I know. Insert royal threat here. I'll be ready."

She waved and was gone, so she wasn't in the room to see him smile.

Victoria scanned her wardrobe, not sure what was appropriate for a formal ceremony. She went with a simple dress that was very classically elegant. Pale blue fabric, wide belt, boat neck, matching heels that had taken her weeks to find and a white leather clutch.

She put her hair up, added nearly real pearl earrings and a thin gold chain bracelet. She walked into the foyer of the palace with five minutes to spare.

Kateb stood talking to several old men. The elders, she would guess. He looked good—very princelike, despite his simple clothes. It didn't seem to matter what he was doing—he always appeared royal. Was it in the blood or the result of years of training?

She studied his profile. The side with the scar was to her, but the slight twisting of his face no longer bothered her. The scar was a part of him, a reminder of a difficult time. Nothing more.

She waited off to the side, watching him. She hadn't meant to admit she was lonely—the words had just slipped out. Yusra was friendly enough, but even she kept her distance. There was no one to just hang with and the person Victoria knew best—namely Kateb—had made it clear he didn't think much of her. It did not make for a fun day.

Nearly as bad was that she wanted to be with him again. *Be with* in a man-woman kind of way. She wanted to kiss him and touch him and make love until they were both breathless. Not that he was interested. Irrational blame seemed to be even more effective than a cold shower.

He looked up and saw her, then gestured her over.

"Very nice," he murmured as she approached. "And no one can see your butt."

She smiled.

He introduced her to the other men. Their names blurred. Then they were all walking out to the front of the palace where several Land Rovers were parked.

"We're driving somewhere?" she asked as Kateb held open the rear door for her. A man was already behind the wheel.

"It isn't far. The nominating ceremony takes place in the arena."

Who knew? "What kind of arena? Big sports facility where they hold trade shows or more stone and Rome Colosseum?"

He sat next to her and closed the door. "The latter."

"I can't wait to see it."

The Land Rover began to move through the village. There were very few people on the street. Those who were waved at the vehicle. A few tossed flowers toward the hood.

"So you're going to be nominated," she said. "Does the king know?"

"I spoke to my father this morning. He is not happy."

Not a surprise, she thought. Kateb was in line for the

El Deharian throne. If he accepted the nomination, he would be abdicating his inheritance, in essence turning his back on his heritage. It wasn't something to be done lightly.

"Did you explain this is what you really wanted?" she asked.

He glanced at her. "The king is not interested in what I want."

"He's disappointed. I'm sure he sees your decision as a rejection of him and what he has to offer. Gee, the throne of El Deharia isn't good enough. That kind of thing. But in his heart, he wants you to be happy. You're his son."

"*Your* father isn't interested in what makes you happy."

"I know." Her presence here was proof of that. "But he's not like other fathers. His heart belongs to the cards, not to any one person. The king loves you." She touched his arm. "He'll get over it."

"You sound very sure."

"I am. I've heard him speak of you. There is so much pride and love in his voice. This will get better."

He squared his shoulders and faced front. "Thank you."

"You're welcome."

She noticed her hand was still on his arm and she pulled it back.

Tension seemed to fill the space. Victoria decided a quick change in subject might help.

"Once you're in charge, are you going to make any big changes? Bring in a mall? A couple of chain restaurants?"

One corner of his mouth twitched. "I had not planned to."

"What about the harem? Keeping that open? You could have your own bevy of beauties calling your name."

"One woman is plenty. Any man who seeks more is a fool."

"Right," she whispered, suddenly deflated.

One woman. A wife. Because Kateb would marry someone and have a family.

It made sense. He would want children—probably sons, but maybe daughters, too. It was the circle of life. He probably had to marry to keep his people happy. Good for him. She would be long gone, back in the States, content in her world.

They'd barely been in each other's company two weeks. It wasn't as if they were friends or anything. She wouldn't miss him. It would be foolish to think she would. Or that he would remember her. Once she was gone, it would be over. Forever.

They arrived at the arena. It was larger than Victoria had imagined, tall and open, with dozens of rows of seats circling a surprisingly large space. An awning shaded the front. As she climbed out of the Land Rover, she could hear the roar of an unseen crowd.

"How many people will be here?" she asked.

"Nearly the entire village," Kateb told her.

He put his hand on the small of her back and guided her through the people milling by the entrance.

Someone jostled her and she nearly lost her footing in her high heels. Kateb reached for her hand and drew her close.

She knew he was only being polite—making sure she didn't get hurt. But she sort of liked her fingers laced with his. It felt right.

They walked around the inside of the stadium, under the seating. Up ahead she saw large wooden double doors with guards.

"Is that where they keep the lions who rip apart the unruly prisoners?" she asked.

"Only on even days. You're safe."

The humor was unexpected. She glanced at him and smiled. He smiled back. Warmth seemed to blossom inside of her, making her feel kind of melty and feminine. If only he would kiss her.

Afraid he would know what she was thinking, she quickly looked away.

"So, um, what happens now?" she asked as they approached the doors.

"Yusra will stay with you through the ceremony. When it's finished you'll be escorted back to the palace. I have assigned two guards to you because there is a large crowd. Don't make a fuss about it."

She paused in front of the double doors. "A fuss? Me? Have we met? Because I'm very easygoing."

"Of course you are."

The double doors opened. She and Kateb walked into a large room filled with thirty or forty people, mostly of them older and male.

The elders, she thought, looking around and feeling a little nervous. Most everyone turned to look her way. Or maybe they were staring at Kateb, she told herself. He was going to be nominated today, not her.

The room itself had food and drinks set up on tables pushed against the wall, and lots of comfortable sofas, not that anyone was sitting. As she watched, a couple of guys started unlocking big doors, then sliding them along the track. The room opened up to the floor of the arena.

Victoria spotted Yusra, who came over.

"Stay with her," Kateb instructed.

"Where are my guards?" Victoria asked.

"Staying out of the way. When it's time for you to go back to the palace, they'll be going with you."

She stared into his dark eyes, not sure what to say. "Good luck" seemed weird and "Have a nice nomination" was stupid. Before she could settle on something else, he moved away.

"Come," Yusra said, taking her by the arm and leading her to a sofa on the side. "We will have an excellent view here and stay out of the way."

Victoria's instinctive protest was that maybe she wanted to get in the way, but she held it in. The elders had lined up, with Kateb at the rear. Everyone looked solemn, as if this was a great occasion. Then she heard music and the arena went silent.

"It is the procession of the elders," Yusra whispered. "They will file out and present themselves. The oldest will call for a leader to be nominated."

"I didn't know there'd be a band," Victoria said.

Yusra smiled. "We enjoy music."

"It's nice."

The men filed out, leaving behind a few big guys she assumed were guards. Yusra had been correct—they could see everything from where they sat.

The men approached a podium she hadn't noticed before. One of them, walking slowly and leaning on a cane, approached. He raised one hand and the music was still.

"Good people of the desert, we, your elders, come before you."

He spoke about the importance of wisdom and how the village had been prosperous. Then he mentioned Bahjat, the previous leader, and how fortunate they had been to know him.

Yusra leaned close. "They will nominate Kateb now."

Victoria turned her head so she could speak into the other woman's ear. "By the way, he said that outfit you left for me wasn't exactly traditional."

"I am surprised."

"Like I believe that. Did you really expect me to wear that here? I don't think the old guys want to be looking at my butt."

Yusra chuckled. "Or perhaps they would like it too much."

Victoria didn't want to think about that. "What did you think you were doing, sending me in there dressed like that?"

"I wanted Kateb to know what he was missing."

Victoria didn't know what to say to that. Apparently Yusra had figured out Kateb wasn't spending his nights in the harem. That he was only counting the days until he knew if Victoria was pregnant or not, so he could send her away.

"Are you trying to trick him?" she asked.

"I'm trying to show him that there are many possibilities," Yusra said. "Do you object?"

"Not exactly," Victoria admitted. Although if she were really a self-actualized modern woman, she should care a whole lot.

"Here it comes," Yusra said, pointing out into the arena. "They will nominate him, then call for challengers."

"What are they?"

"Someone who doesn't agree with the elders' decision. He can challenge Kateb to be the leader."

"What happens then?"

"They fight."

Victoria stared at her. "As in…fight? There isn't a vote?"

"No. They fight with swords."

"Do they know it's a new century? Swords? How do they figure out who wins?"

Yusra looked at her. "Whoever doesn't die."

"What?" Victoria stood. "They fight to the death?"

"Yes."

"And Kateb knows this could happen?"

"Of course. It is our way."

It is a stupid way, Victoria thought, taking her seat again.

She stared out at Kateb. She could see the scar on his face, the regalness of his bearing. She might have made love with him but in truth, she didn't know the man at all.

* * *

A couple of days later, Victoria took a break from working on Rasha's business plan. She'd been walking through the palace, trying to learn her way. Unfortunately there weren't any you-are-here maps posted. Something they should really think about.

She'd already explored the main floor, which was mainly public rooms, and had found that most of the second floor was used for business space. The third floor would be the private areas of the palace.

She took the stairs rather than the elevator, mostly because she was worried about her hips and their pressing need to ever expand. Back in the city, she'd come up with a walking plan, designing circuitous routes that added plenty of extra steps to her day. Until she'd figured out where everything was, she couldn't do that here. Of course there was always the tub in the harem bath. She could start doing laps.

Once she reached the third floor, she paused to get her bearings. The vase across from the stairs was huge and particularly ugly. It would serve as a good reference point when she wanted to find her way down again.

The main building of the palace was basically a square, so it didn't matter which way she turned. As long as she stayed on the main corridor, she would return to her starting place.

She set off to her right, glancing in open doors. There were plenty of guest rooms, a game room complete with pool table, video games and one of those golf stations where you hit the ball into a fabric wall. At the end of the hallway, she saw double doors leading out onto the balcony.

She opened the doors and stepped outside. It was warm, but not oppressive. There was shade from the awning above and an intricate wrought-iron balcony. The El Deharian palace had much the same feature on the living-quarters level. The balcony wrapped around the entire floor. She decided to see if this one did, too.

She walked past many rooms, pausing when she saw one that appeared familiar. After a second, she realized it was Kateb's room and pushed open the door.

The space was as she remembered from that single night when she'd been brought to him. She recognized the furniture and the pile of pillows where they'd made love.

There were signs of him everywhere. In a book left open on a table, the shirt tossed carelessly over a chair. She walked through the bedroom, both nervous about trespassing and yet interested in seeing where he slept.

The room was large, as was the bed and the bath off to the side rivaled that in the harem…minus the swimming-pool tub. She stuck her head in the closet, only to stop and stare at the clothes he had hanging there.

His things were neatly together. A few Western-style suits, shirts, the traditional white trousers. Shoes were lined up on a shelf. It wasn't what he had that caught her attention, but rather what he didn't. The closet was mostly empty, almost lonely. This was not something a man was supposed to have for himself, she thought. It was something he was supposed to share.

Until then she hadn't thought about Kateb's place in all this. He had many responsibilities and now that he had been nominated as leader, there would only be more. He was trusted to help his people grow and prosper. He would be the last voice of judgment for crimes. It was a heavy burden and one he carried alone.

Why hadn't he married? Why was he alone? Shouldn't some desert beauty have caught him by now?

She left the closet. On her way back to the main room, she saw a plain door and opened it.

The room was small—perhaps an office or even a

nursery, she thought. It was difficult to tell. The walls were white, there was no decoration, no furniture save a rocking chair. There were also several boxes and trunks.

The room felt abandoned and dusty. She crossed to a trunk sitting on top of a stack of boxes and opened the top. Inside where folded clothes carelessly covered with photos. She picked up the top one.

Kateb laughed back at her. There was an ease about him she hadn't seen before. His dark eyes radiated joy. He stood next to a beautiful, dark-haired woman, his arm around her, the woman smiling up at him. They looked perfect together.

Something caught her eye. She looked closer and saw a wedding band on the woman's hand. A thicker, matching band glinted from Kateb's finger.

He'd been married, she thought, carefully putting the picture back on the pile and closing the lid. He'd been married and completely in love with his wife. Who was she? What had happened to her?

"She died."

Victoria spun and saw Yusra standing in the doorway.

"She was his wife?"

"Yes. Her name was Cantara. She was the daughter of a chieftain. They'd known each other since he first came here when he was ten. They grew up together."

She was having trouble with the idea, despite the photos. Shouldn't she have heard about this before? Maybe a desert union had been easy to keep secret. "He must have loved her very much."

"She was everything to him," Yusra said, walking over to another trunk and opening it. She reached inside and pulled out wedding photos.

Victoria looked at the laughing young woman in the pictures. Kateb gazed at her adoringly. They were the perfect couple.

"How did she die?"

"A car accident in Rome. It was one of those things. Nearly five years ago. Afterward Kateb disappeared into the desert for nearly ten months. No one saw him or heard from him. We worried he might be dead. But one day he returned."

Victoria dropped the photo back into the trunk and stepped back. "I didn't know."

"He doesn't speak of it. No one does. But everyone worries. He's been alone too long. When he brought you here…" She shrugged and closed the trunk. "We had hoped he had decided to trust his heart again."

"I'm not here because of his heart," Victoria said, not sure why she felt sick to her stomach. She hurried out of the storage room, through Kateb's quarters and out into the hallway.

She didn't know how to get back to the stairs, so she simply started walking. She had to get as far away as she could.

He'd been married. He'd been in love and his wife was dead. How was that possible? How could she not have known?

Now she understood why both Yusra and Rasha had spoken about him being lonely. He was haunted by his painful loss. This explained the distance, the cynicism, the darkness in his eyes.

At last she found the stairs and the ugly vase. She made her way back to the harem and walked out into the walled garden. Once there, she could finally breathe again.

She didn't know why the information changed everything, but it did. It was as if her world had shifted to another dimension. She pressed her hand to her stomach, willing it to calm down.

Until this moment, she'd never considered the possibility of being pregnant, but now she turned the idea over in her mind. Carrying Kateb's baby would mean staying here, haunted by a beautiful woman and her laughter. It would mean being trapped here with ghosts…forever.

Chapter Eight

"Three bids was a starting place," Victoria said as she clicked to the next screen on her PowerPoint presentation. "I can get more, if you'd like. Selling to the home shopping channels on American and European television is really appealing but they would require us to set up meetings and go there with samples. That seems like a complicated first step. This, at least, is easier."

Kateb studied the computer screen. "You are talking about international distribution."

"It sounds more grand than it is. I'm talking about opening up U.S. and European markets."

"Which is international."

"Technically, yes, but it's not like I'm trying to start new manufacturing in China or something. We can test market in a few boutiques in major cities. If we're lucky, get into the trade shows. There's very little up-front cost for this. Rasha has put together a budget and they nearly have all the money they need. Does El Deharia have anything like a small-business administration to help them? I don't think they want to go to their husbands, although I guess they could."

Kateb frowned. "Print out five copies of your business plan and let me study it. I will check your numbers and have my staff research your distributors. If everything is as it appears, I will loan them the money they need to expand."

If she'd been standing she would have fallen over in shock. *"You?"*

He kept his attention on the computer screen. "As you pointed out, diversification is a good thing. Perhaps there are other people who have ideas for small businesses. Word will spread. Bahjat was a good leader, but he didn't believe women had a place in business."

Victoria nearly snorted. "And you do?"

"I am aware that both genders can be intelligent."

"You have a harem."

"As I have explained, it came with the palace."

"You don't seem in any big hurry to convert it to a petting zoo."

"I doubt you would enjoy sharing space with goats and sheep."

"That's true." She saved the file then closed the program. "So you're saying women can be leaders in business. What about in politics?"

He angled toward her. "You wish to govern?"

"Not me, but there must be women who are interested. Will they have an opportunity? Do you think El Deharia is ready for its own Queen Elizabeth?"

"Not today." He glanced at the computer. "Your report was excellent. Well researched, thorough. I enjoyed the graphics."

"Thank you," she said primly, not wanting him to know

how his praise made her feel giddy inside. "I think these women are creating amazing jewelry. They need a showcase for their talent."

"You are providing them that."

"I'm only helping. They're doing the hard work."

He studied her. "You're saying this isn't about you? That if it comes to pass, you won't be the one in charge?"

"No. It's not my business. Rasha is more than capable of managing the business. And I'm guessing that with the excellent wi-fi you have in the palace that there are plenty of teenagers who could manage the Web site. I'm not looking to home in on their show." She rolled her eyes. "Let me guess. You don't believe me. I'm just playing you, right?"

"No, you're not. And I do believe you."

"You'd better."

He looked amused. "Or what?"

"Let's just say you wouldn't like me angry. I'd scare you."

"Yes, I can see that happening."

They were in his office. She was aware of people on the other side of the closed door and the fact that her appointment would end in a few minutes. Although they lived in the same palace, she rarely saw him. Probably because that was how he wanted it. Tonight was the celebration of his nomination and she would be going with him, but she had a feeling there wouldn't be much time alone.

She closed the laptop. "Kateb, I…" What to say and how to say it? "I didn't know you'd been married before. I'm sorry for your loss."

He didn't move, yet she felt him close against her. It was as if a wall came down, separating them. "It was a long time ago," he told her.

"I know. But it must still hurt. I'm sorry."

"You have no need to be."

"I know what it's like to lose someone you love. The pain fades, but it never goes away."

He nodded slightly.

She stood and reached for the laptop. "About the dinner tonight. Am I supposed to meet you there or what?"

"I will come to the harem."

"Yusra said she'd bring me something to wear. After last time, I'm almost afraid."

He gave her a slight smile. "I will speak with her. The clothing will be appropriate."

"Thanks."

She knew it was time to leave, yet she didn't want to go. She wanted to say something else. But what? They were strangers bound by a single night together. He'd already given his heart to another woman and she wasn't interested in love. They didn't belong together. So why did she have the feeling that she would miss him when it was time for her to go?

Kateb found himself looking forward to the evening. Although the idea of a formal dinner didn't appeal to him, he knew that sitting next to Victoria would be entertaining. She would be interested in the events, ask intelligent questions, then make him laugh with her unexpected and humorous worldview.

She was not who and what he would have expected. Her business plan had impressed him. He would guess she'd been an excellent assistant to Nadim and that the other man had never bothered to notice. Just like Nadim had probably never listened to her snarky comments or noticed the sway of her walk.

But Kateb noticed and it drove him crazy. He couldn't be near her without wanting her, which was the downside to the dinner.

"Are you ready?" he asked as he walked into the harem.

"I guess. I'm covered, that's for sure. It's not anything I would have picked."

She walked into the room and turned in a slow circle. "Yes? No? I have a formal ballgown if that would be better."

Yusra had dressed her traditionally, in slim, fitted trousers and a matching long jacket, both in dark gold with delicate embroidery. The jacket buttoned to her neck and the full sleeves came to her wrists. It flared out like a dress, falling almost to her ankles. Yet there were only three buttons, so her midsection was exposed from just below her breasts to her belly button.

The slight view of her pale skin was both unexpected and erotic. It made him want to unbutton the jacket and pull it off, then remove the rest of her clothing. He wanted her naked, wet and moaning. The image was real enough to make him hard.

He ignored his reaction and concentrated on the way she'd piled her blond hair on top of her head. A few curls fell past her shoulders. Her eyes were large and the color of the desert sky.

"You're not saying anything," Victoria told him.

"You look very beautiful."

"Are you sure it's okay? I feel weird in pants." She crossed to a mirror. "I don't know."

"Perhaps this will help." He walked toward her. "Though they are only on loan."

"What are we talking about?"

He pulled a pair of sapphire earrings out of his jacket pocket. She stared at them. The large stones glinted in the light.

"Are those, um, real?"

"Yes."

"The diamonds around them, too?"

"Of course."

She looked at him, then back at the earrings resting on his palm before tucking her hands behind her back. "I don't think so. They're probably eight or nine carats each. If I lose them, I'd have to wash a lot of dishes to pay you back. I don't need the pressure."

She was refusing them? He would have assumed she would jump at the chance to wear such jewelry.

"I am Prince Kateb of El Deharia."

"I've heard that."

"You're my mistress."

"There is a rumor that says that, too."

"Are you trying to be difficult?"

She smiled at him and stepped away. "I appreciate the thought, but I don't need to borrow your jewelry."

"It's not exactly mine."

She laughed. "I don't think you wear it at night when you're alone, but you know what I mean. What I have is fine."

Suddenly he needed to see her in those jewels. "Victoria, I am telling you to wear the earrings."

"And I'm telling you no." She picked up a simple pair of gold hoops.

"Because they are borrowed? If they were a gift, would you wear them?" Was this a way to get something out of him? Another game?

"No, and it's pretty mean of you to even think that. I would worry. I don't need the stress."

"I also have a tiara for you." He pulled it out of his other pocket.

Her eyes widened. "A tiara? Like a princess? I used to have a paper one when I was little. My mom made it for me and glued on glitter. I wore it until it practically disintegrated." Once again she tucked her hands behind her back. "I really couldn't…"

But there was a question in her voice. And longing.

The longing seemed genuine, as did the sadness in her expression.

"At least try it on," he said.

Her breath caught. She reached for it, then gently picked it up, turned back to the mirror and put it on her head.

The diamonds sparkled in her blond hair. She smiled, looking beautiful and regal.

"This is worth having to wash dishes for the rest of my life," she whispered, then met his gaze in the mirror. "Thank you."

"And the earrings?"

"I'll pass."

He shook his head. "You are a very confusing woman."

"I know. Doesn't that just make you want to give me a hug?" She laughed. "Okay. I'm ready. Let's go celebrate you getting nominated."

Kateb stared at her as if she were crazy. Maybe she was, Victoria thought, knowing he would never believe that the earrings, while dazzling, weren't that big a deal to her. She wasn't sure how she felt about borrowing them for the night. But a tiara was different. It made her feel like a princess and for reasons she couldn't explain, connected her with her mother.

"As you wish," he said, and held out his arm.

She tucked her hand into the crook of his elbow. They left the harem and walked toward the great hall.

"They've been preparing all week," she said. "I've been getting in their way, watching them set up. They talked endlessly about the tables. First they tried a big square, but there wasn't enough room. Then they tried rows of tables. In case you were wondering, the palace has a *lot* of tables. I suggested round tables with one long head table. But I'm merely a woman, so they pretended not to hear me. When I went back later in the afternoon, that's what they'd done."

"So you're feeling smug about that."

She laughed. "You have no idea. Want to hear about the menu?"

Instead of answering, Kateb stared at her. "You are most unexpected."

Her insides clenched—the air was suddenly very warm. She felt both happy and shy. "Thank you."

It was their last moment alone. As they turned the corner, she saw dozens of people standing around, talking. Everyone grew quiet as Kateb approached, then they broke into applause. Not sure she belonged in such a special moment, Victoria stepped to the side and clapped her hands as well. Kateb glanced back at her, but didn't slow. She joined the people walking into the great hall behind him.

The elders stood in something resembling a reception line. Kateb went first, greeting them. They each embraced him, obviously pleased with their choice. Victoria wasn't sure what she was supposed to do. She knew she would be seated next to Kateb at the main table, but until that happened, she thought it might be best to stay in the background.

Then she was surrounded and urged forward by the crowd. Before she could get out of the way, she was standing next to the first of the elders, Zayd.

He was old and very small, bent, but with bright, wise eyes. "So you are Kateb's mistress."

Victoria didn't know what to say, so she smiled and hoped it would be enough.

"He needs someone to make him happy. Are you up to the task?"

"I'll do my best," she murmured, thinking that Kateb was actually only interested in counting down the days until he could find out if she was pregnant or not. It wasn't as if he sought out her company or wanted her in his bed.

"You need to do more than that," the elder told her. "You must claim him with enthusiasm and energy. That's what a man wants."

"You make him sound like the last chip on a nacho plate," she said without thinking. "And Kateb's more of a man who does the claiming rather than the other way around."

It was one of those horrifying party moments when the entire room goes silent at exactly the wrong time. Her words echoed in the great hall.

Where was a natural disaster when you needed one? she thought grimly. The old man stared at her for a long time. She couldn't look away, couldn't move and she had no idea where Kateb was or if he'd heard. The way her luck was going, he was standing next to her, ready to snatch back the tiara and lock her up in the harem.

Then the old man began to laugh. He put his hands on his belly and laughed and laughed until tears streamed from his eyes. Conversation around them resumed.

"I've heard of nachos," he said. "Very good. Yes, you'll do." He waved her on.

Victoria quickly made her way through the rest of the line, careful to only smile and not say anything. Kateb was waiting for her when she finished.

When she glanced at him, he raised one eyebrow. Great. Just great.

"You heard," she said.

"It seemed an unusual thing to say."

"You had to be there for the entire conversation."

"Apparently."

He put his hand on the small of her back and guided her toward the head table.

"Are you mad?"

"No. I've been compared to nachos. My life is complete."

She smiled. "You're funny. It's kind of strange, but I like it."

"Thank you."

He held out her chair. As she sat she realized his humor wasn't the only thing she liked about him. She liked that he listened and that, except when it came to assuming the worst about her, that he was fair. He would be a good leader. She liked…him. As a man and maybe even a friend. She respected him.

Which was fine. Better that they get along rather than not. Eventually she would leave and it would be nice to have good memories of their time together.

The dinner progressed smoothly. Kateb endured the elders speaking about him in glowing terms. Their stories were to reinforce their decision but took simple events and expanded them.

"Is there a story about how you slayed the village dragon?" Victoria asked quietly as she leaned toward him. "Or rescued fifteen orphans from a burning building while inventing the Internet at the same time?"

"Later," he told her, enjoying the scent of her skin.

"I like a big finish."

"Then you'll enjoy the dancing girls."

She stared at him. "Seriously? I love dancing girls. I've seen them in the city. Well, I was standing in the back of the room, so there wasn't much detail, but it was very cool. I could never be that graceful."

"You're not insulted?" he asked, surprised by her reaction. "You don't think it's barbaric or demeaning?"

"Why would I be insulted? They go through years of training and it's beautiful to watch. Like ballet, but with sheer pants and veils and different music."

Music filled the large hall. Conversation quieted as several young women walked out in front of the head table. True to her word, Victoria stared intently, as if mesmerized by the entertainment. When the women began to move, she smiled and swayed in her seat.

He did his best to pay attention to the entertainment, but couldn't seem to avoid glancing at the woman next to him. The heat of her body invaded him and no matter how the dancers moved and tried to catch his eye, he could not be interested in anyone but her.

He reminded himself that she might be pregnant and in getting pregnant, she might have tied herself to him forever. He repeated that he couldn't trust her—that she had come to El Deharia for the express purpose of marrying Nadim, and if not him, then someone else with money. He should be angry and not trust her in the least.

But all the words in the world couldn't keep him from remembering what it had been like to make love with her that lone night. The need to touch her again, to please her and be pleased, to hear her breathing catch and feel her soft skin overwhelmed him.

He disliked the sense of needing her so much. Living in the desert had taught himself control. What had happened to it? To him?

Then it no longer mattered. All he could think of was being with her again. The minutes crawled by as the dancers performed. Victoria whispered to him, but he couldn't hear her words. There was only pounding desire that burned through him.

At last the women were still and everyone applauded. The evening had come to an end.

He stood and spoke, not sure of his words, counting on years of attending such events to ensure he said the right thing. Victoria was smiling when he finished, so he must have done well enough. Then he grabbed her hand and started for the exit.

Many people wanted to speak with him, congratulate him, tell him how they were looking forward to his leadership. He nodded and replied where he must, but continued to move toward the hallway.

"Are you all right?" Victoria asked. "Don't you feel well?"

"I feel fine."

"You seem in a hurry."

"I am."

"Why?"

He waited until they were free of the crowd, stepped into an alcove, pulled her close and kissed her.

Victoria didn't know what to think, but the second Kateb's mouth touched her, it didn't really matter. His lips were warm and demanding, taking her with a passion that made her tremble.

He held her tightly, his arms strong and safe. He deepened the kiss, plunging his tongue inside her mouth, making it clear that he wanted her. There was an edge of desperation to his touch, a power that thrilled every part of her. She'd thought they would never make love again and now he was making it known that he wanted to claim her as his.

Even as she kissed him back, their tongues stroking and dancing, she surged against him, wanting to feel all of him. His hands dropped to her rear and squeezed her curves. Her belly tightened, then she leaned in and felt his hardness. She couldn't help rubbing against him, imagining him inside of her, filling her, taking her.

She pulled back enough to see the fire burning in his eyes.

"The harem is closer," she whispered.

He hesitated only a second, but she knew what it meant. Last time they'd been swept away. Last time they hadn't used anything. Neither of them was prepared for the consequences of that act.

"Yusra is very efficient," she told him. "She's stocked my nightstand drawers."

He picked up her hand and kissed the palm. His breath was hot, his touch insistent.

They hurried toward the harem and stepped inside. She led the way to the bedroom she used.

Someone had already turned the lights on low and pulled back the bed. She knew the ever-efficient staff hadn't been reading Kateb's mind. Instead they prepared her room for her every night…as if expecting her to eventually bring home a lover.

And tonight she had.

She turned back to him. He kissed her again, just as insistent as before, his mouth so hungry it made her weak with longing. Even as their tongues mated, he grabbed the front of her gold jacket and jerked it open. Buttons went flying. She shrugged out of the garment. By the time it had dropped to the stone floor, he'd unfastened her bra.

He moved his hands to her bare breasts. Her nipples were already tight and exquisitely sensitive to his touch. He stroked her, lightly brushing the very tips, sending ribbons of fire burning all through her.

When he dropped his head so he could draw one of her nipples into his mouth, she gasped with the pleasure. She clutched his head in her hands, holding him in place, arching her back and whispering for more.

He sucked deeply, pulling her into his mouth. His tongue dueled with her nipple. She was already so wet and swollen, so *ready*. She wanted to squirm and beg, but she liked what he was doing to her breasts too much to ask him to stop. It was an impossible choice—there was so much pleasure.

He moved between her breasts. Wanting filled her until she thought she would faint from the need. At last he dropped to his knees in front of her and reached for the hidden zipper on her trousers. He tugged them down, along with her bikini panties, then parted her swollen flesh and pressed his mouth against the very core of her.

He kissed her intimately, stroking her with his tongue. She was so close already, so near to release, so desperate for him, that it only took a few seconds for her to start shaking. Muscles tensed in anticipation. She could feel herself starting to lose control.

"No," she whispered. Not like this, half dressed, barely able to stay standing.

Once again he seemed to know what she was thinking. He stood and began to remove his own clothing. She kicked off her shoes, pulled off her trousers and stepped out of her panties. He paused to pull a condom out of the nightstand drawer, then they were naked together on the bed, his arousal pressing into her thigh.

She reached down and took him in her hand. His breath caught in a hiss as she rubbed the length of him, then moved her fingers against the tip. He surged against her, only to stop.

"Not so fast," he told her.

He slid down between her legs. She parted for him and tried to hold in a moan as he pleasured her with his mouth.

He moved slowly at first, as if discovering what made her shiver and moan and writhe. He kissed all of her before finding that one swollen spot that thrilled her. His touch was beyond anything she'd experienced, she thought as her body prepared itself for her release. Muscles tensed. She pushed down with her heels and rocked her head back and forth.

Closer and closer. He moved faster, keeping a steady rhythm that made the ending inevitable. Her muscles convulsed as her body shook. Her release claimed every part of her, taking her to the edge and dropping her off the side.

He continued to stroke her with his tongue, more lightly until he'd drawn the last bit of paradise from her body. When she was finally still and able to breathe again, he grabbed the condom, pulled it on and pushed inside of her.

He filled her completely, stretching her, arousing nerve endings until they began to pulse once more. Before she could figure out what was going on, she was coming again. The unexpected release caught her off guard. She clung to him, unable to control her body. Her gaze locked with his as she lost herself in each thrust.

She told herself to look away or at least close her eyes, that this was too intimate, but she couldn't seem to stop staring at him. Neither did he turn away.

He continued to stare down at her, pumping in and out, each stroke sending her into a new level of pleasure. It was beyond anything she'd ever experienced. Each time she thought she was done, she came again until she trembled with exhaustion.

Another thrust and another until his features tightened and she felt the exact moment of his release. She saw everything, the yearning, the relief, the satisfaction. At last he was still and they were done.

Victoria had thought Kateb might simply leave, but instead he lay down next to her and pulled her into his arms. She went willingly, wanting to prolong the moment, to feel him next to her. She told herself it was more about being lonely than needing the man and hoped she was telling the truth.

"Did you mean to do that?" she asked, her head resting on his shoulder.

"Make love with you? Are you wondering if it was an accident?"

She heard the humor in his voice and smiled. "Maybe."

"I didn't slip and fall into you."

"I know. But you didn't want this to happen again."

"Perhaps I can't resist you."

If only that were true.

He stroked her hair. "Why did you offer yourself to me?"

"I told you when it happened. I couldn't let you put my father in jail."

"Because of your mother. Did the promise mean so much?"

She sensed he was genuinely asking rather than questioning her loyalty.

"She was always there for me," Victoria said slowly, closing her eyes and inhaling his scent. "Even though she loved him more than she should have, she took care of me and loved me. No matter how bad things got, I knew she adored me. It helped, through all the other stuff." She opened her eyes. "I made the promise to take care of him because I hoped it would be enough to keep him alive."

"You didn't have that power."

"I was only a few weeks shy of graduating from high school. I wasn't ready to be alone in the world. I had to believe in something."

"You made your way."

"It wasn't easy." She didn't want to think of that time, of the struggles and the fear. Not tonight. "I learned to be strong."

"You were always strong," he told her.

"I wish that were true."

"It takes strength to survive tragedy."

She thought of the boxes in the room next to his. The trapped memories and the pain.

"You must miss her very much," she murmured.

He stiffened slightly. If they hadn't been touching, she might not have noticed.

She put her arm across his midsection. "Don't."

"Don't what?"

"Whatever you were thinking. Leave. Shut down. We can talk about her."

"No, we can't."

"Why not? She was your wife. You loved her and now she's gone. You should talk about it."

"Maybe I have." He stared at the ceiling as he spoke.

"I doubt that. You're not the type. You've kept it all inside. So talk to me. I'm a safe bet."

"In what way?"

"I don't matter."

He turned toward her. "Why would you say that?"

"I don't mean it in a self-defeating way. As soon as you're sure I'm not pregnant, you're sending me back to the city." She wasn't sure exactly why. Perhaps he had initially believed she had tried to trick him, but she doubted he'd stayed convinced of that for long. It was too ridiculous and Kateb was a logical man. "I'm a safe bet. So tell me. What was her name? What was she like?"

His dark gaze locked with hers, as if he wanted to test her sincerity. She didn't look away. Eventually he relaxed. A slight smiled pulled at the corner of his mouth…the corner not touched by the scar.

"Her name was Cantara. She was the daughter of a chieftain and I met her when I was ten and she was eight. She didn't believe I was a prince because I didn't have a crown and she could ride a horse better than me. We became friends. That never changed."

"You're lucky," she said. "Being friends with the person you marry sounds like a great way to make a relationship work."

"It was," he said as he shifted onto his back and tucked one arm behind his head. He kept his other around her. "She understood the desert and understood me. From the time we were sixteen or seventeen, we knew we would be married."

Victoria wondered what it would be like to have that much certainty in her life. To *know* she was loved by a man and to love in return.

"We waited until I was twenty-two," he continued. "My father thought I was too young, but I insisted and eventually he agreed. Cantara and I were married and came to live here."

"You must have been very happy."

"I was. I had everything. A few years later, I had to attend tribal meetings. They can go on for weeks and be very tedious. She decided to go to Europe with a couple of her friends. She was killed in a car accident. She died instantly."

He spoke calmly, as if telling a story about someone else. But she knew there was pain inside of him. Grief that would never fully heal.

"I'm sorry," she said.

"As was I. Time heals."

"Not enough. You're going to marry for duty, not love." He looked at her. "Yusra talks too much."

"That's very possible, but you're not going to stop her."

"Probably not." He touched her hair again. "I will wait until I am leader, then pick a wife who brings power with her. My goal is for my people to know peace and prosperity. An alliance with one of the larger desert tribes will help with that."

"That's your only criteria?" she asked, a little unnerved by his calm determination. "What if you don't like her? What if she smells funny or doesn't have a sense of humor?"

"Ours will be a marriage of duty, nothing more."

"You're expected to have sex with her."

"Not often, if I do not wish."

She sat up and glared at him. "Just enough to get her pregnant? That's romantic."

"It is easier for a man than a woman," he said, obviously amused by her reaction.

"Right. Because all cats are gray in the dark, right? That's beyond disgusting. What about *her* feelings?"

"If she is a chieftain's daughter, she will understand the importance of the alliance."

Victoria stood and glared at him. "Let me guess. She'll be fulfilled by her children and you'll have the harem to keep you company."

"Why are you so angry on behalf of a future wife who doesn't yet exist?"

"I just am."

He dropped his gaze to her body. "You know you're naked, right?"

"Don't try to change the subject."

His attention seem to linger on her bare breasts. "I am simply returning to a subject we were on a few minutes ago."

He moved faster than she would have thought possible, grabbing her around the waist and pulling her back to bed.

She squealed, but didn't struggle too much. Not when his hands were so gentle as he explored her. He kissed her, and at the same time, slipped his fingers between her thighs. All the fight went out of her.

"You're playing dirty," she complained, even as she wrapped her arms around him.

"I play to win," he told her before he kissed her again.

Chapter Nine

Victoria returned to Rasha's house the following morning. She'd printed out several copies of the business plan and hoped they would be as intrigued as she was.

Rasha welcomed her warmly. "We have been excited since your last visit," the woman told Victoria. "Together we have come up with several new designs. Would you like to see?"

Victoria studied the sketches of three pairs of earrings, a couple of bracelets and a pendant. They were all so delicate, yet substantial. Perfectly balanced, amazing pieces.

"I don't know how you do this," she said, touching the paper. "Do you see it in your head first? Does something inspire you?"

Rasha laughed. "Sometimes. Other times I just play around with shapes until one of them speaks to me. It's difficult to explain." She eyed the briefcase Victoria had brought with her. "Good news or bad news?"

"Good news. I have come up with a business plan. I spoke to Kateb about it and he's very supportive." She handed Rasha a folder and left the others on the table. "We can go over this together and then you can discuss it with the other artists. When you've made a decision, let me know and if you want, we'll move forward."

Victoria took her through the plan, page by page. Rasha followed it easily, then frowned when she saw the numbers.

"That is a lot of money," she murmured. "I am not sure how long it will take us to save it. Many years."

"You're not expected to come up with the financing," Victoria told her happily.

Rasha pressed her lips together. "While my husband is very supportive of what I do, he would never… The men of the village aren't as modern as those you are used to."

"Kateb will finance the expansion," Victoria told her. "As a sign of his support. He will offer a low-cost loan. He believes in you and the other women, Rasha. He appreciates your talent and wants you to be successful."

"The prince will finance us? He offers his support?"

Victoria grinned. "That should make this a whole lot easier to sell to the husbands, don't you think?"

"Very much so. How did you convince him? What did you say?"

"I showed him the numbers. He saw the possibilities himself. He's interested in economic diversity. You will be bringing a lot of money into the village, and he respects that."

Rasha beamed. "The prince appreciates us."

She picked up the papers and hurried into the other room where the women gathered around her. She spoke quickly, flipping through the pages. Victoria wanted to point out that Kateb was just a man, like every other. Being a prince was an accident of birth. But they wouldn't see it that way. He was somehow different from them, separated by station and power.

At least he was a good leader, she thought as squeals of excitement drifted to her. The elders had chosen well.

Would his duty wife appreciate that about him? Would she understand that he was mostly alone, having to decide for the many rather than for himself? Would she offer support and comfort? Would she appreciate how he could be kind, but that he didn't want everyone to know he had a bit of a soft spot?

Not her business, Victoria told herself. By the time he'd picked his duty wife, she would be long gone. Which should have made her happy, but didn't.

"We are delighted," Rasha said when she returned. "How do we thank you for your help?"

"I'm having fun with all this. Don't worry about it."

Rasha nodded. "We will design a Princess Victoria collection."

Her own line of jewelry? Could there be shoes, too? "I'm not a princess," she said instead. "Just—you know— the girl in the harem."

"But Prince Kateb must see the treasure he has in you."

"You'd think," she joked, not sure why she felt a tightness in her chest. "Anyway, let's get back to business. I'm going to leave these copies of the business plan with you. Let's talk in a few days and work out the details."

"Yes. That will be wonderful."

They rose and Rasha walked her to the door. When Victoria pulled it open, she saw the same small boy in the yard.

"Go away, Sa'id," Rasha said sharply. "We do not want you here."

The boy's eyes filled with tears as he slunk away.

Victoria was a little shocked by her tone. "Who is he?"

"No one. A child in the village. My sister has a friend who weaves beautiful cloth. Could we sell her work the same way?"

"Maybe." Victoria watched the boy turn a corner and disappear. "Where are his parents? He can't be very old."

"His mother is dead. His father...recently left the village."

Victoria stared at her. "He doesn't have any family?"

Rasha shrugged.

"Who feeds him?" Victoria demanded. "Where does he sleep?"

"That isn't your concern. He will be fine."

Rasha once again brought up the textiles. Victoria promised to think about it, mostly so she could get away and find the boy.

How was it possible that Rasha could be so callous about a child? From all Victoria knew, she was a warm, caring woman. But she'd dismissed Sa'id as if he were a stray cat.

Victoria hurried along the street and turned where the boy had. She saw him sitting in a doorway, wiping his face. He kicked at the stone street with his bare toes.

"Sa'id?" she called softly.

He looked up and smiled at her. "Hello."

"Hello yourself. I'm Victoria."

"You have pretty hair."

"I remember you like it."

He was painfully thin and covered in dust and dirt. His clothes were practically rags. She didn't know much about children, so wasn't sure of his age. Seven? Nine?

She crouched in front of him. "Sa'id, where do you live?"

His smile faded. "I need to go," he told her.

"Please don't. Do you have a home?"

Tears filled his eyes again. "No."

"And you don't have any family?"

He shook his head, then wiped his eyes angrily. "No," he said again, and squared his shoulders.

What the hell was going on? She had seen nothing but kindness from the people in the village. They were peaceful, thoughtful and prosperous. Why would a child be left alone on the streets?

"You must be hungry," she said. "It's very close to lunchtime. I know I'm hungry. Would you like to come with me and get something to eat?"

His eyes widened. "You live in the Winter Palace."

"Yes, I know."

"I can't go in there."

"Why not?"

He shrugged. "I just can't."

"But if I live there and you're with me, wouldn't that be okay?"

He frowned. "Maybe."

She stood and held out her hand. "I say it is and I have very pretty hair."

He smiled. "Okay." He put his hand in hers.

She went around to the rear of the palace, just in case there was some weird protocol thing she couldn't understand. She didn't want to make trouble until she understood everything going on. But she was determined to get the child a meal.

She had barely taken three steps into the kitchen when all the cooks started talking in a language she didn't understand. She caught a few words about dirty hands and sacred space, so she led Sa'id to a small bathroom down the hall. Once they'd both washed their hands, they went into a dining room mostly used by staff. Victoria sat him at a table and went to get food.

When she returned with a tray, one of the maids approached her, then bowed slightly.

"Miss Victoria, you have brought Sa'id to the palace?" The young woman looked frightened.

"Yes. Is that a problem?"

The maid was maybe eighteen, bright and pretty, with an easy smile. It was missing now as she bit her lower lip.

"No, of course not. You are the prince's mistress. I, um, know him. His mother and mine were cousins by marriage. I was just surprised to see him here."

"I was surprised to see him on the street. Do you know why he's living there?"

The woman nodded and ducked her head.

Victoria held in a sigh. There was no point in making her uncomfortable. She would talk to Yusra instead.

"Can you sit with him while I find out what's going on?"

The maid smiled. "Gladly. I am finished for the day. I can take him to my rooms."

"Thank you. I shouldn't be long."

Victoria watched until the maid had spoken with Sa'id. The boy nodded eagerly, then dug into his lunch as if he hadn't eaten for days. Maybe he hadn't.

It didn't take her long to find Yusra. The old woman stood counting linens in a massive closet filled with shelves stacked with towels and sheets.

"The boy Sa'id," Victoria said by way of greeting. "Do you know him? He's living on the street. Apparently he doesn't have any family."

Yusra put down her clipboard. "I know of him. His mother died some time ago. His father stole camels and rather than accept his punishment—he escaped into the desert. The boy bears his father's dishonor." She returned to a stack of towels.

"Wait a minute," Victoria said. "That's it? What does 'bears his father's dishonor' mean?"

"That the boy will be punished in his father's absence."

"Punished how?"

"He is no longer one of us."

Victoria stared at her. "As in abandoned? He gets to fend for himself? He's what, nine?"

"Yes. It is our way."

"Your way sucks. He can starve and no one cares?"

"He must be punished."

"But he didn't do anything wrong!"

Yusra sighed. "There are things you can't understand. This is what we do."

"It's wrong and I won't let it happen."

"You can't stop it."

"Watch me."

The meeting with the head of agriculture normally kept Kateb's interest. Not only did the village produce enough for themselves, but there was plenty to export to the city and even to neighboring countries. This afternoon, however, he found his attention drawn to the sight of Victoria pacing outside the conference room. He could see her every time she passed in front of the open door. She never once glanced inside, but she was obviously waiting for him. If her stiff back and set expression were anything to go by, she wasn't happy.

After five more minutes of her passing back and forth, he stopped the conversation and rescheduled the discussion for later in the week. As the men filed out, she looked at him. He gestured for her to join him in his office.

"What was the meeting about?" she asked as she entered.

"Crop yields for the season."

"How nice. So some people get to eat. Tell me, is there a chart? Do you have to make sure your name is on the list before you get a meal?"

She was obviously furious. He could feel her anger from several feet away. Her eyes snapped with temper and she looked like she wanted to throw something.

His interest in what bothered her surprised him. He would have thought he would easily dismiss her and her concerns without knowing the cause, but that wasn't true. He wanted to hear what had happened and, even more unexpected, he wanted to fix the problem.

He stood from the conference table and crossed to her. After taking both her hands in his, he stared into her blue eyes. "Tell me what is bothering you," he said.

She jerked free of his touch and paced the length of the room. "You won't believe it. Or maybe you will. *I* don't believe it. I like it here. Did you know that? I think it's beautiful and the people are warm and friendly. I love the palace and the architecture and nearly everything. But it's like seeing a dead body in the sun. At first everything is fine, but when you get close you see the crawling maggots. It's disgusting."

"You paint a vivid picture," he told her. "What are you talking about?"

"There's a little boy. Sa'id. Apparently his mother is dead and his father stole camels. Rather than accept his punishment, the man ran off, leaving Sa'id on his own. Now the boy is being punished for what his father did. He's maybe nine and living on the streets. No one is taking care of him, he's not getting any food or medical attention. I'm sure he's not going to school. Where is he supposed to sleep at night? Is he just going to starve?"

Tears filled her eyes. "I don't understand how this is possible. I really liked Rasha, but she dismissed him as if he were nothing. Yusra told me it wasn't my concern. But I can't let a child suffer and die, especially not one right in front of me. I hate this and I hate them for letting it happen."

A single tear spilled onto her cheek. She brushed it away impatiently. "I swear to God, Kateb, if you tell me to leave this alone, I will kill you in your sleep."

He crossed to her and pulled her against him. "No, you won't."

"I'll want to."

"A difference I will cling to in my fear."

She looked up at him, but didn't smile. "There is a starving child in your village. You have to fix this."

"You don't understand our ways. They appear harsh—"

She stepped back and glared at him. "They *are* harsh. Yes, Sa'id's father is a jerk. That's not his fault. He can't change his father. He can't make the situation better."

Just like she couldn't with her father, he thought, seeing this affected her more than she realized.

"The rules are harsh," he said again, "but they serve a purpose. Other adults see the boy's suffering and know their own behavior has consequences."

"So he gets to be an object lesson? I can't believe he is destined to die on the streets. Then what? Who removes his body, or is it left there for the dogs?" More tears fell. "I don't accept this. I won't. This has to be better. Is he the only one? Are there more? Do the people of the village make it a habit to starve children to death? What happened to just loving them? Why is anything about this acceptable?"

Once again he reached for her. This time she came willingly. She leaned against him and cried as if her heart were breaking.

"You can't allow this," she whispered into his shoulder.

He rubbed her back and murmured her name.

So much pain for a child she barely knew, he thought. Victoria wore her heart on her sleeve. She had a softness, a tenderness he had not seen before. She needed protection from the harshness in the world. At the same time, he recognized her compassion gave her an inner strength and a direction he admired. She saw things clearly where others would make excuses.

Finally the tears slowed. He cupped her face, then wiped her cheeks with his thumbs. "Where is he now?" he asked.

"With one of the maids. She's a distant relative. At least I think so. Her mother was somebody's cousin by marriage. I'm not sure."

"Have the boy brought to me."

Her eyes widened. "You'll do something?"

"I will speak to him."

Victoria rushed to the phone and called housekeeping. Less than ten minutes later, the boy was escorted into his office by a young woman.

"Prince Kateb," the woman said, practically ready to fall to her knees. "This is Sa'id."

The boy bowed low. He looked terrified, but stood in the center of the room, obviously prepared to accept his fate.

"Do you know who I am?" Kateb asked.

Sa'id nodded. "You are the prince. I think maybe you will be the new leader, but I'm not sure. I hear people talking, but only some. They don't like me to stay near them."

Victoria took a step toward him. Kateb stilled her with a look.

"I understand you have been living on the streets."

Sa'id nodded. "My mother died and my father…" The boy raised his chin. "My father is a bad man and a coward. He stole camels and when he was caught he ran away. I stand for my family now." He swallowed. "Sometimes it's hard to be hungry but I try to be brave."

Kateb could feel Victoria willing him to do something—to chose compassion over tradition. He knew she would beg for the boy, just as she had begged for her father. Did she ever beg for herself or were all the sacrifices saved for other people? And how could he reconcile the greedy woman who wanted to marry a prince with the person before him? The one in tears over the fate of a small boy she didn't even know.

He looked at the maid. "A place will be made for him, here in the palace." He returned his attention to Sa'id. "Are you afraid of hard work?"

"No, sir. I used to help my father all the time. I'm strong and I don't eat very much." He sounded both hopeful and resigned. As if hope had become an impossible dream these days.

"You will eat as much as you want," Kateb told him sternly. "I need good strong men to serve me and for you to be capable, you must grow. So you will eat all your meals and sleep well and work hard. When you are finished, you will play, as a boy should. Do you understand?"

Sa'id nodded, smiling for the first time since he entered the room.

The maid cleared her throat. "Sir, may I be responsible for Sa'id? I have known him all his life. He's a good boy and we could keep each other company."

"Thank you," Kateb told her. "I will speak with Yusra so that your duties allow you plenty of time with Sa'id." He nodded.

The girl took Sa'id by the hand and led him out of the room. Sa'id paused at the door to wave at Victoria. The second they were gone, she turned on him.

"You made him a *servant*? He's nine and he's going to be scrubbing floors and doing laundry? What about school? What about his education? Or is that not serving the prince well enough?"

"You can be very trying," he told her.

"Ask me if I care."

"I already know the answer." He leaned against his desk. "Does it occur to you to thank me for getting him off the streets? He now has the protection of the prince. That means he will be safe."

"To be a servant."

"For now," he said patiently. "Until I am proclaimed leader, I have minimal power here. As soon as I take the office, I will pardon Sa'id so he can return to the life of a normal boy in the village."

"Oh." The fight went out of her. She looked around the room, then glanced back at him. "You didn't say that."

"You didn't give me a chance. You're very quick to judge me."

"Not you specifically," she admitted. "I'm still angry at Yusra and Rasha."

"Our ways are different."

She put her hands on her hips. "I don't want to hear that again. There's no excuse for what happened to him."

"They didn't like the situation, either, but they know there are reasons."

"Maybe a thousand years ago, but not today."

"Yusra is your friend. Do you wish to be angry with her forever? What about Rasha? Will you no longer support her business because of this? If they do not act as you wish, are they unworthy?"

She crossed her arms over her chest. "You're saying I'm judging them too harshly."

"I'm saying people have different ways. Children frequently illustrate both the best and worst of every culture. Sa'id demonstrates that."

"Are there more like him?"

"Not that I'm aware of."

"When you're proclaimed or whatever it is, will you change the law so children aren't abandoned like that ever again?"

"You ask for much."

"You have much to give."

Cantara would not have asked that of him, he thought. She would have accepted Sa'id's fate as the destiny he must endure. But Victoria would never see it so. She wouldn't care if she expected too much of him. She would fight and nag and work until what she saw as wrong was made right.

The women were so different, he thought, knowing that while he would always love Cantara, she was no longer as much a part of him as she was. Without realizing, he had lost her. Or perhaps time had healed as it often did.

He felt regret and, oddly, hope.

Victoria could not have been more out of place in her jeans and silky shirt, her ridiculous high-heeled boots and dangling earrings. She looked like a woman prepared to go shopping in New York or Los Angeles. Her blond hair and blue eyes set her apart. Her worldview and attitude would always find injustice where others saw nothing out of the ordinary.

"You have a way of tiring a man," he said at last.

"Then go take a nap."

"You won't yield at all?"

"Not on this."

Nothing for herself, he thought, remembering how she wouldn't borrow the sapphire earrings because she was afraid of losing one but she would borrow the tiara because it made her feel like a storybook princess.

"You are a complex woman."

"Thank you."

"I did not mean it as a compliment."

She raised her eyebrows. "Are you trying to distract me?"

"No." He sighed heavily. "When I am leader I will change the law."

He thought she might make him promise, which he would resist. Instead she nodded. His word was enough? How unexpected.

She crossed to him, cupped his face and kissed him. The second her mouth touched his, he wanted her. Need was everywhere, even though the kiss was chaste. Imagine what would happen if Victoria actually tried to seduce him. Or perhaps it was best not to.

"I knew you would make it right," she said earnestly. "When I found out what was going on, all I could think was that I had to get to you. I've never trusted a man before. Not with anything important. So thank you."

She kissed him again and left. He watched her go, then stood alone in the silence.

He felt as if she'd handed him something important. Something precious, although he couldn't say what. Involuntarily he looked at the calendar on the desk. How many more days until they knew if she was staying or not?

He'd planned on her leaving, had hoped to get her out of his life. Now, for the first time, he wondered what it would be like to have her stay.

Except for checking on Sa'id every now and then, Victoria spent the next couple of days mostly keeping to the harem. While she appreciated all that Kateb had done for her, she was still angry that Sa'id had been abandoned by the village—most especially the women.

She understood there were cultural differences involved, but leaving a child to starve on the streets because of actions he couldn't control seemed inhuman. Children were vulnerable enough without worrying about that.

Every time she nearly calmed down, she thought about what had happened and got angry all over again.

While she liked Rasha and Yusra, she couldn't reconcile their actions with someone she considered a friend. As they were pretty much the only two women she knew in the area, that left her by herself for way too many hours a day.

On the third day, she was tired of the harem and went down to the kitchen for lunch. As she turned the corner to head in that direction, she nearly ran into Yusra. The two women looked at each other.

"You are angry," Yusra said, forcing the issue.

"Yes." She braced herself for the fight—for the older woman to say she would never understand the ways of the desert people and so on. It was an argument she could never accept.

"I was wrong." Yusra sighed. "My husband has been gone many years now and still I hear his voice in my head. He would tell me about the old ways and how they must live on. I believed him, and I didn't question Sa'id's fate. No one did. It was not something we wanted to see, so we all looked away. It took someone from the outside to remind us of who we are. That we value family and kindness."

It took Victoria a second to realize she didn't have to be mad anymore. "I don't know what to say," she admitted. "I'm glad you see that Sa'id is only a little boy."

"Of course. He's a wonderful child. Rasha and I have been talking. As soon as the prince is made village leader, we are going to ask him to change the law. We will stand firm on this, not leaving until he gives in. Rasha has already talked to Sa'id's cousin about taking them both in. Her children are grown and her house more empty than she would like."

The relief tasted sweet, Victoria thought happily.

"Kateb is already planning to look into changing the law, but I'm sure he'll be happy to hear that there are others who agree with him."

"Good." The older woman tilted her head. "So we are friends again?"

Victoria smiled. "Yes. Of course. I'm sorry we fought."

"The fault is mine. I got so used to what has always been."

"We all do."

"Come," Yusra said. "You were on your way to lunch. We will eat together and talk about all the ways we can change the laws."

"Kateb won't like that," Victoria said with a laugh.

The kitchen was crowded with many of the staff. When Yusra and Victoria entered, the large room went silent. Victoria felt everyone looking at her.

"Ignore them," Yusra said, approaching the buffet set up against the far wall. "They will get used to you. It will take time. Word is spreading about what you did to help Sa'id."

"Not everyone will like me butting in."

"Perhaps, but those who don't will not have the courage to say anything. At least not to your face."

Victoria laughed. "Then I'll try to enjoy them talking behind my back."

"As you should."

After lunch Victoria made her way to the library. She wanted to see if there were any lists or catalogues for all the artwork in the palace. Someone had to figure out what was there and make sure it was taken care of. Or at least insured. Assuming insurance was available. Did Mutual of El Deharia exist?

She'd been in the large, open room dozens of times. As she walked in, she saw someone else was there, which was odd. Usually she had the space to herself. Then the man turned and her heart skipped a beat or two before resuming a slightly elevated rhythm.

"Kateb," she said, then realized her voice was a little breathless and cleared her throat. Lately she'd noticed a bit of a quiver when they were together. A slight vibration deep inside her belly. It was more than just the longing to be with him. It was something else she couldn't name and didn't want to study too closely.

"I didn't think you were the library type," she said.

"I am not," he told her, looking amused. "Yusra informed me you were heading this way and wished to speak with me. Apparently she believes you have the power to summon me."

Yusra had called him? She wasn't ready to share what they'd discussed at lunch an hour ago, but unless she came up with a credible substitute, it appeared she was going to have to.

"She's right," Victoria told him. "You have appeared."

"How fortunate for you. What is it now? Emancipation for cats? A school for the sheep?"

"Don't mock my good works," she told him, even as she smiled. "Yusra said I was right about Sa'id."

"Words I'm sure you never tire of hearing."

"That's true."

"What did you promise at lunch? Are my people to ask for more money? Better weather?"

She hesitated. "I haven't had a chance to organize my thoughts."

"Has that stopped you before?"

"Not really. Okay. More than fifty percent of the staff at the palace is female and most of them have children. The time their shifts begin and end follow a tradition that dates back a couple hundred years to when mostly men worked here. It would be helpful for them to start and stop at different times. Some want to come in early, others late. It seemed reasonable to me. Also, the male secretaries make more than the female secretaries. I can't begin to tell you how much that annoys me, speaking as a former assistant." She paused for breath.

He stood, looking at her, still appearing amused.

"Are you taking this seriously?" she asked.

"Very."

"Did you want to write any of this down?"

"Not really. You will remind me of anything I forget."

"That's true."

"What else?"

"The textiles. I don't know how to get them into the marketplace. I was wondering if I could write some of the other princesses in the area. They've been doing the royal thing longer and might have some suggestions. From my research, Princess Dora of El Bahar seems like a great place to start. But I think I need your permission to do that."

"You have it."

As easy as that? "And the other stuff?"

"I will address it when I am leader."

"The first week?"

"Perhaps the second. I will be busy the first week."

She wanted to launch into him but held back. He'd been more than reasonable about Sa'id, so she wasn't going to assume it was something silly.

"With what?" she asked.

"As leader, I am granted twelve virgins. I may pick one as my wife or not. The others live in the harem, there only to please me." He smiled. "So I will have my hands full for the first few days."

"Your hands full?" She didn't care that her voice came out as a screech. "With twelve virgins? Are you serious? I don't believe this. There are serious matters of government for you to consider and you want to talk about twelve virgins?"

She was just getting started when Kateb began to laugh. He crossed to her, put his hands on her shoulders, then kissed her.

"I am pleased that Nadim never did raise his head from his work enough to notice you. Had he seen the spark of life you carry inside, he might have decided you would do for him and he would never have appreciated your fire."

He kissed her again, this time lingering against her mouth until she felt her knees go weak.

She didn't understand. "You're not marrying one of the virgins?"

"No. Nor will I take them into the harem."

"Then why bring them up at all?"

"Because you make it so easy, Victoria. You should learn to control your temper."

She glared at him. "What I should do is throw one of these books at your head."

He laughed again. "You won't. The books are rare and you might damage one."

"That's true."

He touched her cheek. "Your points on the women are well taken. And yes, write Princess Dora and ask her advice. She is a strong, intelligent woman. You have much in common with her."

He left her standing in the middle of the library, feeling as if she'd been struck by a train. What had just happened? What exactly had he said? And why had she reacted so strongly to the thought of the other women? Why should she care?

She walked toward the shelves of books, only to stop.

Her breath caught in her throat as the truth…and horror… of the situation crashed into her.

She cared because sometime since arriving at the Winter Palace, she'd fallen in love with Kateb. She'd given her heart to him and now he had the power to destroy her.

She knew love was for fools and now she'd become one. Her fate, her very future, rested on a single moment of chance. If she was pregnant, she would stay in the presence of a man who would never believe she loved him. And if she wasn't pregnant, she would be forced to leave. There was no middle ground, no happy ending, no way to win.

In this game, the deck was truly stacked against her.

Chapter Ten

The workrooms of the house shined as if they had been polished for days. Kateb supposed they had. The launching of the Internet site for the women's jewelry business had attracted many of the village's residents and Rasha would want to impress her neighbors.

Kateb circulated through the crowd, looking for Victoria more than listening to those around him. He was one of only a few men in a sea of women, which should have made spotting her difficult. However, her blond hair caught his attention.

He saw her speaking with one of the artists. Victoria said something and the other woman laughed. She had her profile to him. Her features had become familiar, yet were still beautiful. He knew that beneath her professional suit lay curves that could drive a man to madness, but he did his best not to think of them. Better to focus on the event itself and on the orders coming in through the Web site.

"Prince Kateb." Rasha appeared at his side and bowed. "We are so honored that you have come here this afternoon. You have made so much of this possible. We will always be grateful."

"You have a thriving business," he told her. "I support that."

"Thank you." She waved to the crowded room. "This is all because of Victoria. She is the one who saw the possibilities. She worked tirelessly. Did you see her business plan? It was very impressive. I believe she went to college."

Rasha's voice sounded wistful. While many El Deharian women attended college, it wasn't that common for girls in the village. They went to local schools, then frequently married young and started a family.

"She has a two-year degree," Kateb said. "In business."

"Imagine what she could have done if she had been able to earn a four-year degree. Education is so important."

"Do you have daughters?" he asked.

"Yes. Two. They are eight and ten."

"Will they go to college?"

She looked surprised by the question. "They are intelligent girls with dreams, of course, but I am not sure…" She cleared her throat. "No woman in my family has attended college and my husband, while supportive, would not see the need."

A fairly typical reaction, Kateb thought. The men had to be *shown* the need.

Rasha excused herself to see to her guests. Kateb returned his attention to Victoria. What *would* have happened to her if she'd gotten a four-year degree? Would she have entered a management training program in a large company? If so, by now she would be close to running the world.

He smiled at the thought. Perhaps the world would be a better place for it.

Yusra moved toward him. "You have seen enough?"

He checked his watch. "I have been here nearly twenty minutes."

"Plenty of time for them to notice your presence, sir."

He wondered if Victoria would agree. Regardless, he was ready to return to the palace. Yusra walked with him. Once they were in the street, she paused.

"Victoria is already working with the women who weave. Did you hear? She had written Princess Dora of El Bahar to ask for her help in marketing the fabric. She has a meeting scheduled with the old men who carve. They, too, wish to sell on the Internet."

He hadn't heard that. "Interesting. She has started a revolution."

"In only a few weeks. You must be very proud of her."

Pride implied he had some influence or control over her actions. She had done all this on her own.

"She isn't like the women of the desert," Yusra said earnestly. "At first I thought of her only as someone to please you. To help with the loneliness. I know you still miss Cantara, and that is as it should be. Victoria would be a distraction. But she is more. She saw the truth about Sa'id when the rest of us turned away. She sees the possibilities."

Kateb stared at the old woman. "What is your point?"

"That it will only be a week or two until we know if she is carrying your child. It seems unlikely, which means you will be letting her go. She has given much to us. So what is to become of her? Will she return to the city and work as Nadim's assistant? Take another job? Surely she deserves more."

He hadn't thought about the future, about what would happen after he knew if Victoria was pregnant or not.

Yusra was right—he couldn't send her back to work for Nadim, assuming the position was still open. What would she do? Return to America? Work for someone else?

"I think you should help her find a rich husband."

He stared at the older woman. "What?"

"She needs a husband. You've seen her around the palace and today. She's a woman who was born to give her heart. She should have a family, many children, a place to belong. She respects your opinion. She would listen to you."

"Then you don't know her at all," he said, annoyed beyond reason and not sure why. Getting Victoria married made the most sense. But to introduce her to someone? To know that man would claim the treasure of her heart and her mind? Impossible. "She would never agree to an arranged marriage."

"You wouldn't have to tell her what you were doing. You could guide her."

"Right. Until she figured out what I was doing and threw a large vase at my head."

"You need to do something. She can't be sent out in the world unprepared."

Victoria was many things, but unprepared wasn't one of them. Still, he understood Yusra's point. "I will consider the matter," he said, and walked away.

Victoria knocked on Kateb's open office door, then walked in. "You sent for me?" she asked, not sure if she was going to have a little hissy fit about that or not. After the successful opening party the previous day, she was feeling pretty darned good about everything, but being "sent for" was still a tiny bit annoying.

Kateb stood and motioned to the sofas by the window. "Yes. I have several things to discuss with you, although

I'm sure first you wish to complain about the fact that I sent for you."

Could the man now read her mind? "I have no idea what you're talking about," she lied. "You asked to see me and here I am."

"Because your job is to serve?"

"Something like that."

His dark gaze drifted over her face. "You're not a very good liar."

"Hardly a bad quality. So you sent, and I'm here. What do you want?"

"Rasha and the other women are very pleased with all you did, as am I."

"I enjoyed helping them. They have a great business and they can use the extra money."

"Their husbands support them."

"For now. What happens if one of them does the 'I divorce thee' three times or however it works?"

"That is not El Deharian law."

"Fine. One of the men goes on a camel-stealing rampage and his wife is kicked out onto the street. My point is a woman having an independent income is good for everyone. She gets to feel a little self-worth, and he has to stay in line."

"I suspect you are more interested in him staying in line."

She smiled. "Maybe, but you get what I'm saying, right?"

He sighed. "Equality for all."

"Is this where you point out that I'm difficult?"

"No. I'm saving that for later. I had an interesting conversation with Rasha yesterday. She reminded me that not enough women from the village and the desert tribes are going to college. It is not traditional for them to attend and many fathers are uninterested in doing much more than acquiring a good husband for their daughters."

Victoria sprang to her feet. "Are you aware of what a waste that is for your country? There are brilliant minds not being used. Who knows what could have been invented or discovered or improved? But *no*. Let's keep the women home for breeding. This just really pisses me off."

"I would not have guessed."

He leaned back against the cushions, obviously more amused than annoyed. She narrowed her gaze.

"You told me this on purpose," she snapped.

"Yes."

"You knew it would upset me."

"I suspected you would have a strong reaction."

"Do you want me to threaten you or something?"

"No. I wanted to see if you were as passionate about the subject as I had thought you would be."

"And?"

"And you should sit down again."

She wasn't sure what he was up to, but she sat back on the sofa.

He leaned toward her. "It has come to my attention that you have one of those brilliant minds we were speaking of a few minutes ago. You see need and you fill it, especially where women and children are concerned."

His assessment pleased her. "Men can take care of themselves. They've had the money and power for centuries."

"We won't debate that now," he said. "Don't try to distract me from what I want to say."

"I don't know what that is. How could I distract you?"

He stared at her until she squirmed. "Fine," she muttered. "Talk away."

"Should you not be pregnant, what are your plans when you leave here?"

The unexpected question made her glad she was seated. She didn't want to think about leaving, about being away from him, never seeing him again. But was there a choice? He'd already shortened her time with him from six months to one.

The thought of leaving in a week or two hurt more than she could have imagined and she knew the reason. Love made her vulnerable. Love made her want to stay always, made her want to promise anything so he would keep her around. She'd actually considered offering to be his mistress permanently, knowing he would be marrying someone more appropriate. Which meant she had to leave as soon as she was free. She couldn't stay here and be a doormat for a man who wouldn't or couldn't love her back.

He waited patiently while she struggled to remember the question. What *were* her plans?

"I thought I would go back to the States," she said at last.

"Eager to leave the desert?"

"Not really. I like it here. But once we're..." She cleared her throat. "Once it's time for me to go, I will. I don't think I'd be comfortable staying in El Deharia on my own."

"You don't want to continue to work for Nadim?"

"No."

"Good." He leaned toward her. "You have a gift, Victoria. You have the ability to help others achieve their dreams. Is that something you have considered?"

"Not really," she said slowly. Where was he going with this? "I've been saving since I came to El Deharia. I didn't have many expenses and I've always been a frugal shopper. I thought I might take the money I have and start my own business. I just haven't figured out what. I'll think about what you said. About helping others."

"I would like you to consider it seriously. With the right

funding, you could change people's lives. If you had the financial backing, imagine what you could do."

She didn't like the sound of that. "Is that what you're offering?"

"Yes. I would like to start a company with you. Perhaps a non-profit foundation that gives money to people who wish to start a business but don't know how. You would assemble a staff of experts who would help them with every aspect of what new entrepreneurs need. From coming up with a business plan to hiring, advertising, dealing with tax regulations."

She hadn't expected anything like this and didn't know what to say. "It's a wonderful opportunity," she murmured, torn between the excitement of being able to make a difference and the reality of being tied to Kateb. It would be easier for her peace of mind to simply walk away and never have to deal with him again.

"I would like you to consider it," he said. "You could establish the main office anywhere in the United States. Where would you like to live?"

Did he have to sound so eager to get rid of her? "I'm not sure."

"There is time for you to decide. And while we are on the subject of your future…"

He paused and for the first time since she'd met him, she had the sense that he was hesitating. Almost uncertain. "Kateb?"

He gave her a reassuring smile that did everything *but* reassure her.

"I would like to find you a husband. You have said many times you're not interested in love, but you would like to be married for reasons of security. I am acquainted with many intelligent, successful men. Men who would be interesting and good husbands, without expecting all the emotional messiness that can make relationships difficult. If you wish, I can compile a list of potential suitors and arrange introductions."

For the second time in as many minutes, she was glad she was sitting. Every part of her body had simply stopped working and had she been standing, she would have fallen to the floor.

He wanted to find her a husband? Was that the same as helping her look for a lost shoe or lip gloss? Did he plan to put an ad somewhere or hold interviews?

But that wasn't what hurt, she thought, as cells slowly came back to life and her heart started beating again. No, the cold ache that spread through her was about how easily he said the words. He didn't care if she was married to someone else. It might even make him feel better about the past month. She was a problem and once he'd fixed the situation, he could move on with a clear conscience.

None of this was about *her*. She wasn't a person who mattered. She wasn't significant to him. She'd fallen in love with a man who had no trouble thinking about her married to someone else.

Until that moment she hadn't realized a fantasy had lived inside of her. One that said Katcb would turn around and actually see her. That he would recognize they were good together, that they could be happy. That he loved her.

She knew Yusra would tell her to be flattered. The prince taking so much interest in her future meant that he cared a little. Perhaps she was on the same level as a prized broodmare or a priceless painting. Something to be worried over and put in a safe place. But not anything he missed when the object was gone.

"Victoria? Are you interested in a husband?"

He sounded so calm, she thought, hurt turning to anger because anger was so much safer. He sounded reasonable.

"What else is on the table?" she asked, glaring at him. "A private plane? A small island? A large island? How about my picture on a stamp? Can I have that? Maybe a few jewels? You don't have to buy me off."

"What's wrong? I'm not trying to buy you off. I want to take care of you."

"By finding me a husband?" she shrieked.

"Why does that offend you?"

She supposed in time she would take comfort in the knowledge that all men were equally stupid. Even princes.

She stood and stalked to the door.

"Victoria, why are you angry?"

He sounded genuinely confused, as if he couldn't imagine what was wrong.

She didn't answer the question. She kept on walking. When she reached the harem, she looked around for something to throw, then grabbed a pillow off the sofa and tossed it.

The act wasn't the least bit satisfying. She eyed a vase on a stand, but knew it could be priceless and her snit wasn't worth destroying that. When she heard someone enter the harem, she braced herself for another encounter with Kateb, but found Yusra instead.

"What's wrong?" the other woman asked. "You are pale. Are you ill?"

"Kateb is an idiot," Victoria yelled, then walked to the far end of the room. She needed to move. Maybe if she went far enough, she could leave all this behind.

"What has he done?"

"He wants me to run a foundation to help women start their own businesses. Which is great. It's a dream, really, one I didn't even know I had."

Yusra stared at her. "And?"

"And he wants to find me a husband."

The old woman didn't look surprised. "You need to be married."

"What I need is to kick him in the head. He's going to find me a husband. Isn't that nice? One who won't mind that I was briefly mistress to a prince. But is that a bad thing? Won't it make a great cocktail-party conversation? This is Victoria. My wife used to sleep with an El Deharian prince."

Her eyes began to burn. There was no way she was crying over Kateb. He didn't deserve it.

"Our ways are different," Yusra began slowly. "He is showing that you are important to him."

"By giving me to another man? Oh, yeah, I'll just stand here and feel the love."

"Would you rather he walked away without considering your future at all?"

"No." She wanted him to realize she cared about him. She wanted him to be unable to let her go. "No. That would be worse."

"Then why is there a problem?"

Yusra wasn't an idiot. She'd been around a long time and Victoria was pretty sure she'd already figured out the problem.

"You're going to make me say it, aren't you?"

Yusra nodded.

Victoria opened her mouth, then closed it. "I won't. It's not true. It'll pass. Like a stomachache."

Yusra clicked her tongue and shook her head, then walked into the harem's back rooms.

Victoria trailed after her. "I'm not in love with him. That's what you're thinking, aren't you? Well, I'm not. He should honor his original bargain and keep me around for six months. That's only fair. Then I'd leave. I want to leave, but only after I've paid my debt."

Yusra straightened a few towels. "Yes. I see how this is all about your guilt."

"Not guilt exactly," Victoria mumbled. "I don't love him. That would be incredibly stupid. Love is for fools."

"It is a woman's destiny to love. It is how we are made. You can try to deny the truth, but it is the same as a turtle believing he can fly. No matter how he resists reality, he will always crash back to earth. So it is with you. You love him."

Victoria sucked in a breath. "I don't want to."

"Does the wanting or not wanting change what is?"

"Don't get all mystic on me."

The older woman moved next to her and patted her shoulder. "It is good that you love him."

"He wants to send me away and marry me off to someone else."

"Perhaps."

There was no "perhaps." It was real and it was happening. "I don't matter to him at all. Or at least not enough." Not enough for him to want her to stay.

"He doesn't know how you feel."

Victoria held up both hands, palms out, and took a step back. "I'm not telling him. No way. Not me. Are you serious? Give him that much power? I don't think so. Did you know Cantara? Am I anything like her?"

"No. She was very traditional. She had lived in the desert all her life. She was the love of his youth. He needs a new love now that he is a man."

The words made her heart ache, Victoria thought sadly. She would give anything to be that woman. The one he cared about. The one he wanted to be with for the rest of his life.

"He can't have loved someone like her and then care about me. We're too different. I don't bring anything to the relationship. No tribal connection, no power base. He said his marriage will be political."

"What else is he going to say? That he doesn't want to love and lose again? What man admits that? Tell him how you feel. What is the worst that will happen?"

She shuddered. "He'll reject me."

"Is that the worst? Or is it spending the rest of your life not knowing?"

Kateb knew that Victoria was angry, but he had no idea why. She was a most complicated woman, he thought grimly as he made his way to the harem two days later.

He had offered to take care of her for the rest of her life. He would give her a great business to run and find her a good husband. What more could she want? But was she grateful? Of course not.

Worse, he had sent for her twice and she had ignored him both times. No one kept him waiting—and he would tell her that explicitly.

He stalked into the harem, letting the door bang shut behind him.

"Victoria," he yelled, "you will appear before me this instant."

"I'm not a ghost," she yelled back. "I don't appear and disappear. Right now I'm busy. Go away."

Incensed, he followed the sound of her voice, then wished he had not when he stepped into the harem bath and found her in the middle of the large pool.

The swirling water did little to conceal her nakedness from him, which would make it difficult to have any kind of serious conversation. But to retreat now would be to show weakness. He would simply ignore her firm, round breasts and the curve of her hips. He wouldn't notice her long legs or how she'd piled her hair on top of her head. He was strong and powerful. A sheik who ruled the desert. He could resist a mere woman.

"I sent for you twice."

She stayed under the water, looking both wary and defiant. "So I heard."

"I am Prince Kateb of El Deharia. You will come to me when I summon you."

"Apparently not."

"You are my mistress."

"For the next few days, then I'm gone. Or are you going to change the rules again? For all your claims of greatness, your word isn't worth much."

Fury erupted inside of him. "You dare to speak to me this way?"

She actually yawned. "I'm sorry. What was the question?"

He wanted to grab her and shake her. He wanted to pull her out of the pool and…and…

Desire swept through him. Blood pooled in his groin. Wanting was stronger than anger, and he resented her power over him.

As he stood well above her and was fully clothed, he should have had the advantage. So why did he feel she was winning?

"I don't understand," he said at last. "Why are you angry? I'm offering to help."

"I don't remember telling you there was a problem."

"I want to ensure your future."

"By finding me a husband?" she asked, obviously outraged.

"Yes, but if you don't want one, I'll give you money instead. You'll be taken care of." Shouldn't that make her happy?

"What is the going rate for a month of mistressing?" she asked in a tone that warned him she was not pleased. "It's more than I would have thought. I'm surprised more women don't seek the position, as it pays so well."

He frowned. "Your sarcasm is unnecessary."

"It feels pretty necessary to me. Now please, go away."

"You keep saying that, but I will not until this is settled."
He drew in a breath. One of them would have to be rational
and as the male, the job fell to him. "Victoria, I know your
past and how it has shaped you. My goal is to make sure you
never worry about money again. Why is that a bad thing?"

"Why are you so concerned?" she asked, sounding almost reasonable.

"Because you are someone I appreciate. When I first
brought you here, I had a different view of you. I was
wrong. You should respect that."

She stood. The water came to her waist, leaving her
breasts bare and wet. His need for her grew.

"You mean I'm not the money-hungry bitch you'd first
imagined? You no longer have to worry about punishing
me? I've become worthy of your attention?"

He sensed the trap but couldn't see it. "Yes."

"What a terrific statement about my character. I would
think you'd be more worried about my pregnancy. But
you don't seem to be at all."

Still wary, he said, "It is unlikely. As you said, it was
one night."

"So you might have overreacted," she snapped. "What
a shocker. But we have to be sure, because it's a royal child.
Let's see. If you're going to give me money and a husband
for a month of being your mistress, what would you offer
if I had a child? The moon? The Arabian Sea?" She turned
her back on him. "Just leave."

Kateb stared at her bare shoulders. He genuinely didn't
understand her. "What do you want?" he asked. "How can
I make you happy?"

An interesting question, Victoria thought sadly, wondering how he would handle the truth. Would he listen? Would

he consider the words? Or would he use them against her, ripping her heart from her body and trampling it into dust?

She climbed out of the bath and grabbed a towel. After wrapping it around her body, she tucked in the end and crossed her arms over her chest.

A defensive move, perhaps, but necessary. It was that or grab something like a shield from the wall. Odds were, Kateb wasn't going to react well to what she had to say.

Not that fear would stop her. Yusra had been right. In the end, not knowing would be worse than rejection. At least that's what she would tell herself later.

Unless Kateb surprised her. Unless he had feelings for her, as well. The possibility and hope gave her courage. It would have to be enough.

"I don't want you to find me a husband," she said quietly, staring into his dark eyes and wishing being around him didn't make her heart beat faster. "I don't want your money. You're not responsible for me. When I leave, I'll be on my own. It's better that way."

He frowned. "What *do* you want?"

She sucked in a breath. "You. I want this to be real." She glanced around the room. "I'm not interested in being your mistress. I want it all, Kateb."

She could feel herself shaking. She did her best to hide it. "I've fallen in love with you. I didn't mean to. It just happened. You're not what I expected at all. You're a good guy. I like being with you. You make me laugh, even when you don't mean to, and that's pretty cool. I want us to be together. I want—"

"Stop," he commanded, darkness invading his eyes. "Do not say any more."

"Kateb?"

"No." He stepped back. "No. This is not allowed. This is not to be. Love between us is impossible."

Knowing this could happen still hadn't prepared her for the pain that sliced through her. Her heart fell still. And yet she was able to stand before him.

"I don't have a choice," she whispered.

"Neither do I. I don't want your love. I have never wanted it. Not from you or anyone."

She swallowed. "Why does it have to be bad?"

"Because I will never love you and I will never seek love. We'll never be together. You're the last woman I would ever marry. It is over. Done."

He walked out of the harem. She waited until she was alone, then sank onto the floor. The stone was cold and hard, just like the man. She curled up and waited for the tears.

She told herself that at least she knew and in the knowing there would be peace. Eventually. Just not today.

Chapter Eleven

Kateb had little interest in meeting with the elders before the ceremony that would make him leader, but there was no way of getting out of it. While his father, the king, could be difficult, Mukhtar was only one man. The elders were many, opinionated and stubborn. Although they wanted to discuss several issues facing the village, he knew there was one major topic on their collective minds. Getting him married.

While the position of leader was earned rather than inherited, having a wife and children was a statement about a man's character. Kateb understood the importance and intended to comply with tradition. What he didn't like was having to talk about it. Especially now.

Although he hadn't seen Victoria in two days, she was with him every moment. Her words taunted him, angered him, left him unable to sleep. He was furious with her and he couldn't say why.

He made his way to the elders' chamber and was announced by the guard at the door. Once he was named leader, he would take his place at the head of the table, but for now he stood, a mere visitor in the room where all important decisions were made.

Zayd, the spokesman for the group, acknowledged him with a nod and rose.

"You are well, Prince Kateb?" he asked politely.

"Yes. Thank you. The elders?"

"We are old," Zayd grumbled. "And getting more so by the day. We summoned you here to speak of your future, and by association, our own."

Kateb said nothing. When it was his turn to speak, they would tell him.

"We have reviewed your plans for the village. Your economic policy is aggressive. Perhaps too aggressive."

"The old ways still work," another man said, glaring at Kateb. "You think you're going to change everything in a week? It doesn't work that way."

Kateb waited for the nod from Zayd, indicating he could respond.

"The old ways are the backbone of our way of life and our financial success," Kateb told him. "I have no desire to change that. I seek only to add muscle to an already strong economy."

He explained a little of what he had in mind, then outlined his goals for his first year. They listened, which was the first step in getting them to agree.

"This is all fine and good," another man said, his voice wispy with age, "but what about getting married? Cantara was a flower of the desert, to be sure, but it has been five years, Kateb. You mourn her and those emotions speak highly of you. But it is time for you to marry again. Tradition demands it and so do we."

"I agree," he told them. "I am ready to take a wife."

The elders looked at each other. Usually they were expert at keeping their opinions to themselves, but they were obviously surprised by his agreement.

"Do you have a preference?" Zayd asked. "Have you chosen someone?"

He thought of Victoria, who had proved to be an unexpected treasure. Until a few days ago.

"No one," he said clearly.

Zayd raised his eyebrows. "I see. Then appropriate candidates will be brought to the village."

"I will choose from among them."

There were a few whispered comments between the elders. One of the old men stood.

"What of Victoria? Does she remain in the harem?"

Not if she wasn't pregnant, he thought, still angry at her and still unclear why. It didn't matter that he wanted her, that she pleased him in so many ways. It was impossible for her to stay.

Unless she was pregnant. If she carried his child, then he would have no choice but to keep her. The law was clear—a royal child could not be taken from the country without permission of the king. And Mukhtar would never give it. Victoria would never leave her child, trapping her in the village until the child was an adult.

What would that be like? Having her so close? What would he do with her?

The most logical solution was to retain her as his mistress. To keep her close and…

No. That was not his way—not when he was to marry. Which meant the easiest solution was for her not to be pregnant. That would be best for everyone. But if she did have his baby, all her strength, her determination, her intelligence would flow through to that child.

"I have not yet determined what will become of her,"

he said, unwilling to explain the reason. They should know about the pregnancy within the week. "I will decide after the final naming ceremony. If she is to leave, the potential brides must wait until she is gone."

He might not trust her, but he wouldn't insult her by having to live with them in the harem. If she was pregnant…he would deal with that problem later.

The elders spoke to each other, then Zayd stood again. "Do you wish to marry the American? While tradition and political expediency suggest you take a desert bride, Victoria has proven herself many times over. Her work with Rasha has already brought glory to the village. She was wise about Sa'id when others didn't see anything but a shamed child. She is strong and compassionate. If you wish to marry her, we have no objections."

Marry her? Impossible. To marry her would be to…

And then he understood the anger burning inside of him. He knew why her words had offended him and made it impossible to speak of anything else.

She wanted to stay here. She'd finally found a place she could call home. But instead of coming to him and saying that, instead of discussing the possibility of changing their deal, she'd tried to trick him with words of love. She'd thought that he would believe her.

She didn't love him—she only wanted the security he could provide. This wasn't about him at all.

"I will not marry her," he said clearly.

Zayd sat back down. "I see." There was disappointment in his voice. "As you wish."

"If she wants to stay in the village, we can find her another man to marry," one of the elders said.

"No." Kateb would not allow that. "No one else may have her."

He understood the ridiculousness of his position. He

didn't want her and he didn't want anyone else to have her. To explain would be to give too much away. But she was not to be trusted—he knew that much. Love. How dare she claim that emotion? How dare she try to trick him with her perfect face and body, with her humor and intelligence. It was just like a woman.

But he was too smart for her and he would find a way to punish her. Then he would walk away and leave her with nothing.

Victoria sat in the harem garden and wished there was a way to get a really big lock on the door. One that would keep her trapped inside forever. She could live out her life here, just her and the parrots and maybe a dog. A dog would love her, no matter what. A dog wouldn't walk out on her after she told it she loved it. A dog would care.

Unlike Kateb, who had casually ripped out her heart, then set it on fire in front of her. She'd never been in love before, she hadn't known how much it could hurt. She'd told the truth, offered him all that she had and he'd walked out on her. He'd brutally rejected her and the hell of it was, she couldn't just walk away. Not yet.

But soon.

That morning, she'd felt the first dull ache, low in her belly. Right on time, she thought sadly, knowing that in a couple of days she would get her period and have the proof Kateb required to let her go.

Once she told Yusra, how long would it take until she was gone? An hour? Two? Then she would face the drive back to the city and the endless plane ride home. Once she arrived in the States, where would she go? She didn't have any family except for her father and she didn't want anything to do with him. There was no reason to return to

Texas. She could go to Los Angeles or Denver or Seattle. Maybe she could get lost in New York.

Possibilities that should have excited her, but all she could think about was how much she would miss Kateb. She ached for him, would do anything for him and didn't have a clue as to how to get him to listen.

She raised her face to the sun, then stiffened when she heard footsteps in the harem. They were fast and determined. Her heart began to beat quicker as anticipation raced through her. She had it bad, she thought sadly. She would rather see Kateb, knowing he was angry and would hurt her, than be without him. Apparently she was going to have to spend some quality time with self-help books when she got home.

He swept into the garden, then stalked toward her.

"We must speak," he announced.

"As you wish."

His dark eyes seemed like weapons as he glared at her. She ignored that and his obvious fury, instead studying him so that she would never forget the breadth of his shoulders or the scar on his cheek.

She thought about offering him a seat, but he seemed to have too much energy to be still. She waited as he paced on the stone path in front of her. He would have to be the one to speak first—she'd said everything she could think of already.

"You should have talked to me," he told her, his gaze narrowed. "You should have said you were interested in staying here. If you'd been honest with me, we could have come to terms." He stopped and looked at her as if she'd called down a tornado to wipe out the village. "Instead, you tried to deceive me."

For a few seconds, she thought he might be speaking some alien language with clucking sounds and squeaks.

Then the words rearranged themselves in her head and she was able to make sense of what he'd told her.

The meaning sank in slowly, forcing her to her feet. The ache disappeared behind a big wall of mad.

"Are you saying that if I'd come to you and said 'hey, big guy, I'm thinking this is working for me. Let's get married,' that you would have been fine with it? That you would accept a business deal from me but because I told you that I was in love with you, all bets were off?"

"Yes," he said tightly. "Of course."

"Of course?" she shrieked. "You're more comfortable with someone who only wants to use you? But someone who wants to give you her heart is a problem? Let me tell you, you're going to be in therapy for the rest of your life. That's beyond crazy. It's twisted on a level I can't even joke about."

She walked to the end of the path, then spun back. "Did it ever occur to you that I was telling the truth? That I *am* in love with you?"

He didn't say anything, but then he didn't have to. The answer to her question was clearly visible on his face. It was in the way he wouldn't look at her anymore and the tension in his shoulders.

"It didn't," she said quietly, as the fight went out of her. "You never thought it was possible."

He started to say something, but she raised her hand. "Don't," she told him. "There's nothing you can say. No. Wait. I take that back. There's one thing. Tell me one thing I've done to *you* to make you think that. One thing. Give me a single example, because I'm not seeing it. Who have I hurt here? Where was I mean or difficult or so incredibly awful that you can't even consider I might have feelings for you? Was it with Rasha? With Sa'id? Did I steal? Did I lie? Did I not give everything I had here?"

"I can't." His voice was quiet.

She turned away. "Right. You can't. But that doesn't matter because this isn't about me. It's easy to make me the bad guy because then you don't have to look at yourself."

"Victoria, do not go there."

She tried to laugh and couldn't. "You can't stop me, Kateb. I don't care that you're the prince. What I care about is that you're the man I fell in love with. But you're still caught up in what happened five years ago."

She spun to look at him. "It was bad. Probably the worst thing anyone could go through. The death of a loved one is devastating. I know that. I respect that you loved Cantara. But you're not dead yet and you still get to have a life."

"That is not for you to say," he yelled. "I don't want this. Any of it. I will marry again because it is my duty, but it will be different. A marriage of convenience."

"Is that what Cantara would have wanted? Would she be proud of you right now?"

"Do not speak of her!"

"What do my words change? She was your *wife*, Kateb. You knew her best. Is this her doing or yours? Not loving again won't bring her back."

"Nothing about this concerns you."

"Of course it does. I love you and you don't believe me. How is that not my business? I'll accept that you don't share my feelings. I get that maybe this isn't what you wanted. But that's not what you're telling me. You're turning your back on the rest of your life because you're afraid of getting hurt again."

"No!"

"Yes. That's all this is about." The more she said, the more she knew it was true. "I love you, Kateb. You can refuse to listen, but that doesn't change the truth. I love you enough that I want you to be happy, even if it's not with me. But what you're doing…it's wrong. Worse, it's cowardly. You're afraid to try again because you don't want to risk losing someone else you love. But what is life if not taking chances? Those who try the most get the most. You're sentencing yourself and your future wife to years of mediocrity, all because you're terrified."

She drew a breath. "I thought those in charge were supposed to lead by example. Apparently that's not you. Do as I say, not as I do? Is that what you'll tell your children?"

He didn't fight back. Victoria would have taken him on but he didn't give her the chance. He simply left and she was alone, again.

It hurt just as much as it had before, but it wasn't as shocking. She wanted to believe that he would get it. She wanted to trust in love and hope and everything good. But how could she fight a man who wouldn't try?

She supposed the good news was that he had to have some feelings for her or he wouldn't be so angry about her telling him she loved him. If he didn't care at all, he would probably keep her around. Having her love him would feed his ego, if nothing else.

But knowing he had feelings and refused to acknowledge them only deepened her sadness. She touched her aching stomach. She had days, maybe hours, and then it was finished. In the beauty of the warm, sunny afternoon, she heard the ticking of an invisible clock. One that counted down until everything was over and she would never see Kateb again.

Bowing to the inevitable, Victoria started packing that afternoon. When it was time, she wanted to go quickly. No lingering, no regrets. Then the healing could begin.

She would have to go to the market one last time. She wouldn't tell anyone she was leaving, but the visit would be her private way of saying goodbye. Maybe she would spring for another pair of earrings from Rasha's store. Something to remember the village by. She wouldn't need anything to remember Kateb. She had a feeling she would never forget him.

She'd filled one suitcase and was starting on another when Yusra burst into the harem. The old woman looked wild-eyed. Victoria's first thought was for Kateb.

"What's wrong?" she demanded. "What happened?"

"There's a challenger. I don't know who."

Victoria looked puzzled. "Challenger for what?"

"Kateb as leader." Yusra grabbed her arm. "We have to do something."

"I don't understand. What does a challenger matter?"

Yusra pressed her free hand to her chest, as if trying to catch her breath. "It is tradition. Kateb was nominated and in the time up to him being named, someone can challenge the elders' decision."

"That can't make the elders feel good," Victoria said, still not sure what the deal was. "So how do they decide? Do people vote?"

"No. This is a challenge, not an election. They fight for the position."

Fight? As in…the fight Kateb had described to her before? "How?"

"With broadswords. In the arena. The winner is the next leader. The winner is the man who survives. The fight is to the death."

Chapter Twelve

"No!" Victoria said loudly. "No. He can't fight to the death. What if he's defeated?" Kateb dead? She wouldn't be able to stand it. "There has to be something we can do."

"There isn't. Tradition demands the fight."

Victoria couldn't breathe. "Who's challenging? What if he's some gladiator guy who's been practicing for years." She fought against tears. "We have to stop it."

"We can't. If Kateb refuses the challenge, the other man wins. Worse, Kateb is shamed and branded a coward." Yusra patted her arm. "He is a worthy fighter."

"And when was the last time he fought to the death with broadswords? Not lately, I'm guessing. What is wrong with you people? Can't you just hold an election like everyone else?"

"If Kateb survives, you can talk to him about changing the laws."

"Assuming he survives." Panic swirled inside of her. "What can we do?"

"Nothing."

"I can't stand this," Victoria told her. "What if the other guy gets in a lucky shot and wounds him? Then he kills him and it's not right." Kateb couldn't die.

Yusra hesitated.

"What?" Victoria demanded. "What are you thinking?"

"If either man is injured, another can take his place. A sacrifice."

Nothing was making sense. "What are you saying?"

"If Kateb were injured, the challenger would kill him unless someone else stepped in. The sacrifice then fights in Kateb's place."

"Or dies," Victoria whispered.

"Yes. The fight only ends with death." She drew in a breath. "We worry too much. Kateb is strong and skilled. He will prevail."

But what if he didn't? Victoria couldn't stop thinking about him lying in the dirt, bleeding to death. That wasn't what she wanted for him.

They would have to find someone to take Kateb's place if he were injured. But who would be willing to die for him? And even if someone were, how could she ask one man to give up his life so someone she loved could go on living?

"I really liked living here right up until now," she said. "I swear, if he comes out of this alive, I'm making sure the law changes. I don't care what it takes." Her stomach clenched with a cramp reminding her she didn't have much time to make that happen.

The elders' chamber was in an uproar. Everyone spoke at once. Kateb listened to the sea of voices and disregarded the words. They weren't important. What mattered was defeating the challenge.

"This is most unexpected," Zayd said. "He waited until nearly the last day."

"He is a boy," another man called. "Kateb will defeat him easily."

Zayd looked at Kateb. "The boy fights for revenge, Kateb fights for what is right. Who is to say how it will end?"

Kateb met the old man's gaze and understood his point. The challenger had planned this moment for years. There was power in making something happen. There was power in avenging a father.

"I do not take the challenge lightly," he said. "But there is no question of the outcome."

The old men nodded. "So it will be," one of them called.

The door to the chamber burst open and Victoria rushed inside. Kateb couldn't remember a woman ever entering the room before. The men all stepped back, as if afraid of her. She ignored them and came directly to him.

"What is wrong with you people?" she demanded as she approached. "What's wrong with something as simple as an election?"

There were tears on her cheeks and worry in her eyes. He forgot that he was angry with her, forgot that he was counting the moments until he could send her away. He held out his arms and she rushed into them, then hugged him as if she would never let him go.

"I won't let you do this," she mumbled against his chest. "I'll tie you up and beat you with a stick until you agree that hiding isn't such a bad thing."

She smelled of sun and flowers. Her body was familiar and tempting and he wanted her, as he always did. He kissed the top of her head before saying, "You wouldn't respect a man who let that happen."

"I'd get over it."

"I would not."

She raised her head and looked at him. "Kateb, you can't do this."

"I must. I want to."

"Fight with broadswords. Do you even know how?"

He smiled. "Yes. I am very skilled."

"And here I thought I was hot stuff because I can build a Web site. Why is this happening?"

Zayd inched closer. "Perhaps you would like to speak with Victoria alone. Somewhere else."

She glanced at the older man. "What's going on?"

"You've violated the sanctity of the elders' chamber. Women aren't allowed."

She rolled her eyes.

He chuckled. "Come," he told her. "We'll speak of this in the harem."

Victoria went willingly. She wanted to be alone with Kateb and the elders' worried glances made her want to slap them all. Probably not the best plan, considering she might have to go to them and beg for Kateb's life. She was determined to do something to stop the madness—she just had to figure out what.

They walked to the harem. Once they were inside, seated on one of the overstuffed sofas, she turned to him.

"Start at the beginning and talk slowly. Why is there a challenger? Who is this guy? Is it personal? It feels personal."

He touched her face. "Why would you say that?"

"Because it's coming up at the last minute. What? He woke up this morning and thought 'Wouldn't it be cool to fight Kateb to the death?' I don't think so. If this wasn't about you, why not challenge back when you were named? Or go to the elders before? Everyone knew they were going to pick you."

"You are right. It's personal. His name is Fuad and he is the son of the man I killed."

She gasped. Her gaze settled on the scar on his face. "When you were kidnapped?"

"Yes. Fuad's father had come up with the plan to kidnap me and hold me for ransom. When I tried to escape, he and I fought." He rubbed his cheek. "He nearly won, but in the end, I prevailed. He was killed, the men with him imprisoned."

"His family shamed," she whispered, remembering what had happened to Sa'id after his father had only stolen a few camels. "So this Fuad grew up seriously mad at the world in general and you in particular. He wants revenge for his father."

"Most likely."

That was bad. Even worse than she'd thought. "You can't fight him. He's got something to prove."

Kateb looked weary. "I will not take pleasure in defeating him. Fuad is only a boy. Maybe eighteen or twenty. But it is the law."

"The law is stupid."

"Saying that doesn't change it."

"So you change it."

"I will. After I am leader."

"Which means you first have to kill Fuad."

What if you don't? Victoria didn't say the words, but she couldn't stop thinking them. What if Kateb was killed?

"You worry too much," he told her.

"This isn't the 1800s. No one does this. You have to make it stop."

"I will. I will win."

"With a boy's death on your hands?"

"There is no other way."

"There has to be. Go to the king," she begged. "Tell him. He'll forbid you. There's no shame in that."

"The king will not interfere with our ways and neither will you." He touched her cheek again. "Fear not. I am good with a broadsword and I will practice."

"You have two days."

"That is enough time."

Was it? Wouldn't Fuad have been practicing for the past ten years?

Fear clawed at her chest, making it hard to breathe.

She wanted to tell him to just stop and be sensible about all this, but knew he wouldn't listen. He would go forward with the challenge because it was how things had always been done. He was a prince of the desert. He didn't fear death, but then he wouldn't be the one left behind.

She leaned forward and kissed him. She needed his mouth on hers, his hands touching. She needed to be with him one last time. Before the battle. Before he sent her away.

She'd thought he might resist. That he might still be angry, or assume the worst about her. But he cupped her face and kissed her back.

She parted for him immediately and he swept inside. Their tongues brushed together in a dance that was as arousing as it was familiar. Only Kateb, she thought, trying not to cry, even as her body melted against his.

He broke the kiss and pulled her to her feet. She went willingly and he led her into the bedroom.

If he saw the open suitcases on the floor, he didn't say anything. Instead he drew her to the side of the bed, then kissed her again.

His mouth was more gentle this time, offering as well as taking. He swept his hands down her back and over her hips before sliding them up to her breasts. There was a tenderness in his touch. Almost loving.

They quickly removed their clothes, then fell together on the bed. When he would have slipped his fingers between her legs, she shook her head.

"Just be inside of me," she whispered. "That's what I want."

The connection, she thought, determined to remember everything about this moment. The joining.

He put on a condom, then knelt between her thighs. She reached for him and guided him inside.

She was already wet and swollen. Just the thought of them making love was enough. Today she wasn't interested in her own pleasure, although it was there. She wanted to be one with him.

He filled her slowly, stretching her. Nerve endings quivered with delight. Wanting burned through her and she found herself moving with him, unable to resist the call of her release.

But she held back, focusing instead on staring into his eyes. On every part of what they were doing.

Without warning, he pulled out and rolled onto his back. Then he urged her on top. She straddled his hips and eased herself down on his erection. While she braced herself on her hands, he reached up and cupped her breasts. Then he smiled.

"Better," he whispered.

He teased her nipples, which made her insides clench. Powerful desire swept through her, making it difficult to think about anything but how he made her feel. She rode him up and down, finding the perfect rhythm, wanting all he had to give her.

He continued to tease her breasts. They stared at each other. She felt herself getting closer, pushing harder, going faster. He moved with her, driving in deeply, filling her until she had no choice but to give in.

Her climax claimed her with a rush of pleasure that

made her cry out. He dropped his hands to her hips, guiding her up and down until he, too, groaned. They came together, eyes locked, both panting and straining. It was the most intimate moment of her life.

When they were done, he rolled them onto their sides, facing each other. She traced the length of his scar. Tears filled her eyes.

"I love you," she whispered, then dropped her fingers to his mouth. "Don't say anything. I'm not expecting anything from you."

Emotions battled in his eyes, but she knew that she wouldn't be the winner. There was too much doubt. His reluctance wasn't about her, it was about losing again. She couldn't promise that wouldn't happen and even if she could, he wouldn't believe her. He would rather be alone than risk love. Worse, he wouldn't admit any of this. Instead he pretended he couldn't trust her. How was she supposed to fight that?

"I'm not pregnant," she continued. "I'll be getting my period in the next day or so."

"How do you know?" he asked, his mouth moving against her fingers.

"I feel bloated and I want to eat my weight in chocolate. I just know. I'm staying through the challenge, and then I'll leave." Unless he wanted to stop her. Unless he wanted to take a step of faith and admit he cared about her.

Instead he stood and dressed. Then he left without saying anything.

Victoria and Yusra carried the large, dusty book to the closed doors. The book was huge—nearly the size of an end table and about as heavy as a water buffalo.

"I can't go in there," Yusra told her, looking nervous. "It's the elders' chambers. No women are allowed."

"I survived my visit," Victoria said. "If you don't want to stay, that's fine, but I need your help carrying in the book."

"All right." Yusra glanced around the corridor. "If the guards see us…"

"They won't do anything. I'm the prince's mistress and you're here because I insisted. We're fine."

She balanced her half of the book with one arm and used her free hand to bang the door knocker three times. They staggered back a few steps and waited.

Seconds later someone slid open a space at eye level. "Who seeks the counsel of the elders?"

"This was so much easier when the doors were just open," Victoria muttered, then looked at the man. "Victoria. Tell Zayd it's about the challenge. I have a solution to the problem."

"You are a woman." The man sounded outraged.

"Really? Huh. Who knew? Look, this stupid book is heavy. Tell Zayd what I said. If you don't, I'm going to make a sharp keening sound that will not only break glass, it will make you incapable of ever pleasing your wife again. Now *go!*"

There was a rustling sound, then the mini door slid shut. Seconds later the big door on the right creaked and opened. Two guards rushed out. For a second Victoria thought they were on the verge of having a close encounter with the dungeon, but the guards took the book from them and walked back into the chamber.

"I guess we're supposed to follow," she said.

"You go first," Yusra told her.

Victoria smoothed the front of her tunic. She'd chosen a conservative, traditional long-sleeved shirt over loose trousers. She was covered from neck to toes, not wearing any flashy jewelry, and she'd pulled her hair back in a

French braid. She hoped that by looking serious, the elders would take her seriously. They were her last hope.

The men were seated at a U-shaped table, all staring at her. Some looked curious while others were obviously having fantasies beginning with the words *off with her head.* She ignored all of them except Zayd. Not only was he in charge, but from what she'd heard, he was the most reasonable.

"Thank you for seeing me," she said, and bowed. "I'm here because of the challenge."

"How can you help?" Zayd asked.

"By offering myself as Kateb's sacrifice."

The men all looked at each other, then stared at her.

"Impossible," one of them said forcefully.

"Not really." She did her best to smile. "Look, we all know this is about revenge. I have a bad feeling about this kid. He wants to win in a big way, in front of a lot of people. What if he cheats or something? Do you really want him as your leader? Do you want him in charge? Kateb is the best man for the job and while I think we should have a serious discussion about women and leadership, this isn't the time or place."

The men started speaking with each other. Zayd held up his hand for silence. "Go on."

"So if Fuad tries something, Kateb could be hurt. If he is, I rush onto the field as the sacrifice, Kateb is saved and we all go home."

Zayd stared at her. "The fight is to the death."

She didn't actually want to think about that. "Okay. Everyone goes home but me." She cleared her throat. The death part wasn't her favorite.

"You're a woman," one of the elders said.

"Why does everyone keep saying that, like I don't already know?" She turned to Yusra. "This is your part."

The older woman motioned for the guard to bring her the book. She flipped through it and began to read. It wasn't in English, so Victoria pretended interest until Yusra pointed at her, indicating she'd reached the relevant part.

"As you just heard, there's no requirement for the sacrifice to be a man," Victoria said. "You can't refuse me. It's my choice. I will be Kateb's sacrifice."

"Do you know how to use a broadsword?" one of the elders asked.

"No, and I'm not going to try."

Her plan was simple. If Kateb got into trouble, she would run out and throw herself on top of him. She just hoped Fuad was really good and made the ending quick.

"I'm not going into the arena to defeat him," she said. "I'm going to die."

Conversation exploded. Yusra closed the book, then moved close and took her hand.

"You are very brave."

"I'm a lot of things, but brave isn't one of them." She didn't want to do this, but it was the only way she could think to keep Kateb alive.

"Kateb will never allow this," Zayd said.

"He's not going to know. The only way I get involved is if something happens to him. If he's injured, he won't be in a position to stop me. Between now and then, none of you are to tell him."

A very old man stood and pointed his finger at her. "Why would you do this?"

Talk about a stupid question, she thought. "I love him. I don't want him to die."

Zayd nodded slowly. "As you wish, Victoria. You may be Kateb's sacrifice. Yusra will bring you to the arena and keep you from him. We will say nothing."

"Thank you," she said, both relieved and terrified.

"I hope Kateb knows the treasure he has in you," Zayd told her.

"Me, too." The problem was he didn't—and by the time he figured it out, she would probably be dead.

Chapter Thirteen

Kateb walked to the harem. No matter how he busied himself with broadsword practice, with matters of government, he couldn't forget Victoria's words. Her claims to love him, her telling him that he was afraid to try again. Afraid to lose.

She was wrong, of course. He was Prince Kateb of El Deharia and he feared nothing. But he would miss her.

It had taken him most of the night to see that. Victoria was different from any woman he'd ever met. Cantara had been…comfortable. They had understood each other. She had been the love of his youth. What was Victoria?

Still unsure of the answer, he walked into the harem and called her name.

"Back here," she yelled.

He followed the sound of her voice to the bedroom. As he entered, his gaze settled on the bed where they had made love the previous afternoon. Where she had offered him her heart. Where he hadn't know if he should take it or not. Could he trust her?

All her suitcases stood closed and ready to go. She was dressed in jeans and a T-shirt, obviously prepared to leave.

"I got my period," she told him with a shrug. "I'm leaving after the challenge."

She had warned him, but he hadn't listened. Now, disappointment coursed through him, making him want to demand she be wrong. If she *had* been pregnant, it would have been so easy. He could have forced her to stay. He would have had more time to determine what was real and what was only as he wished it to be.

"You have no interest in the challenge," he said.

"I want to see you win."

"There is no victory today," he told her. "Not with Fuad. I have no desire to kill him."

"Do you have to?"

"If he begs for mercy, I can release him."

"He's here for revenge. He's not going to beg."

"I know."

Kateb walked to the doors leading out to the garden. "There are times when the old ways weigh on me. When they feel like chains dragging me down."

"When you're the leader, you can break the chains."

"When," he echoed, then turned to look at her.

Sunlight touched her face, as if it, too, would miss her presence here in the village. His gaze dropped to her feet, where she wore high-heeled boots that had no place in anyone's wardrobe.

"Stay," he said without thinking. "Stay here with me. You love me, so marry me."

She pressed her lips together, then swallowed. "Why?"

He had hoped for a happy response, for her to throw her arms around his neck and kiss him until he had no choice but to take her to bed. But Victoria was never easy…or predictable.

"Because you want to. Because I enjoy your company. Because I will take a wife and you are the one I choose. You will pass your intelligence and determination on to our sons. Our daughters will share in your beauty and wit."

"Sometimes you're a serious sexist pig," she said with a sigh. "You'd think that would bug me." She looked at him. "Do you love me?"

"No."

"Do you believe I love you?"

Did he? To believe would be to trust. And trust was the first step in wanting more. To give his heart again? Losing Cantara had devastated him. What would happen if he lost Victoria?

"I'll take that as a no," she murmured. "I'm leaving after the challenge."

"If I forbid it?"

"You're not the boss of me. Not anymore. It's better, Kateb. You know that. Staying here, loving you knowing you didn't trust me or love me would only make me miserable. I'm not the type to suffer in silence. We'd fight all the time and neither of us wants that."

Emotions rushed through him. He grabbed anger because it was familiar. "I will lock you in the harem."

"No, you won't. You're not that guy."

"You know nothing about me."

"I know everything." She moved toward him and raised herself up on tiptoe, then kissed him. "That's why I love you. Now go fulfill my warrior-prince fantasies. Yusra says it's quite the outfit."

He ignored her humor. "I am not finished with the conversation."

"Sorry, your time is up. You have to be at the arena."

She was right and that irritated him. "We will discuss this later."

"I hope so," she whispered. "I really hope so."

Victoria waited until she was sure Kateb was gone before leaving the harem and going to Yusra.

"That is what you are wearing?" the older woman asked when they met up by the kitchen door.

"Yes. Why?"

"I had thought something more traditional."

"If I'm going to die today, I'm going to be comfortable. And you have to admit, the boots are spectacular."

Yusra hugged her. "I have been praying for your safety."

Victoria hugged her back. "Good. I've been doing a little quality time with God myself. I really hope this works out."

"You can change your mind. The elders will understand."

"I can't," Victoria said, even though she was starting to feel sick to her stomach. "I have a bad feeling about this whole thing. I need to make sure Kateb is all right. I can't explain it."

"You love him. There's nothing to explain."

They started for the arena. "If this goes badly and I don't make it," Victoria said, "feel free to spend the next fifty years making him feel guilty."

Yusra's laughter turned into a hiccup-sob. "I will. I promise."

"Good. I mean, I want him alive, but there's no reason he can't be suffering at the same time."

They moved into the main road leading to the arena. It was a hot, sunny day and everyone in the village had come to see the challenge. There was a festive air to the afternoon. Carts stood along the side of the road selling everything from frozen treats to bottled water.

When they reached the main entrance to the arena, she

and Yusra turned left and went toward the doors leading under the seating. The guards there let them in at once. They were led to the elders' chambers, where Zayd greeted them.

"Is that what you're wearing?" he asked Victoria.

"Get off of me. Yes. I'm wearing jeans."

"But you're a woman."

She looked at the kindly older man and knew it would be rude to wrestle him to the ground in front of all his friends.

Zayd seemed to sense her impatience. "It is of no matter," he said. "You are here as the sacrifice?"

"Yes, on behalf of Prince Kateb." This was the official part of the event. Yusra had told her what to say. "I don't want him to know," she added. "Not unless I'm needed. If everything goes great and he defeats Fuad, then no one tells him, ever. Right?"

Zayd nodded. "As you have requested. We honor the wish of the sacrifice."

"Then I'd really like a donut."

"What?"

"Never mind." It wasn't as if she could eat. Nerves danced in her stomach. She was terrified and not just for herself. What if something happened to Kateb?

Kateb waited by the field. The broadsword felt good in his hand, heavy and powerful. It wasn't pretty to look at. No jewels adorned the handle and the blade itself showed marks from battle. But he had trained with this sword while growing up, learning the art of battle, as dictated by tradition. He and the sword were old friends. There was trust between them.

The sun was bright, the arena full, but he ignored everything around him. There was only himself and Fuad and the possibility of death.

He did not want to kill the son. The death of the father had been bad enough and that man had been a criminal. To end a young man's life for no reason save revenge was a waste he couldn't stomach.

Sometimes tradition sucked, he thought, smiling as he heard Victoria's voice in his head. She was right. He would change the law, but it would be too late for Fuad.

Tonight there would be great celebrating. Kateb would be named leader and stories would be told about his victory. How many would see the falseness of the moment? How many would mourn Fuad?

Victoria would understand. She would know he would sleep uneasily for some time, hating what tradition forced him to do. She would chase away the ghosts.

Except she would be gone. She was leaving after the challenge. Forbidding her from leaving would change nothing. She wouldn't listen. He could hold her prisoner, but to cage her was to cage something wild and beautiful. In time she would wither and he couldn't bear to see that.

"Impossible woman," he growled.

She would agree to that, too, and point out the solution was simple. All he had to do was love her. Admit what he felt in his heart. Give her all that he was, and she would be his.

To risk himself again that way? To believe in her, in them, and know that at any second, she could be gone? It was too much.

But to live without her? What was that, but years of emptiness?

"It is time," the master of the arena told him.

Kateb cleared his mind of everything but the battle to come and stepped onto the field. A cheer shook the arena. The very ground seemed to shake from the sound. He ignored it all, looking at the young man approaching.

"You have grown tall," he told Fuad when they were only a few feet apart.

The boy was now near twenty, muscled and determined. His dark eyes promised death, but Kateb saw past them to a lonely child who had grown up in the shadow of his father's shame. Was this Sa'id in ten years if Victoria had not intervened? Was Fuad what his people had made?

"Prepare to die, old man," Fuad said with a sneer. "Today I will spill your blood and avenge my father."

Old man? Kateb supposed that thirty did seem old to the boy. "Your father kidnapped me and was prepared to kill me. His death was my right."

"I am his son. *Your* death is *my* right."

Victoria would not approve of this circle of violence. She would say that it was stupid and a waste of resources and that if he was really good at his job, he would find a way around it.

"You're not going to listen to reason, are you?" Kateb asked.

Fuad turned his back and walked away.

"I don't want to kill you," Kateb called after him. "Ask for mercy and I will grant it."

Fuad spun and raised his sword. "It is not yours to give, old man. I will kill you slowly. You will watch your life-blood spill on the dirt and have time to know why you die."

Victoria couldn't hear what they were saying, but she didn't like Fuad's body language. He wanted Kateb to suffer. That much was clear. Fuad rushed at the prince, his sword raised. She winced and tried to look away, but couldn't. The sound of metal on metal echoed in the afternoon. Kateb deflected the blow and turned.

Over the next few minutes, she managed to relax. Fuad fought with anger and it made him clumsy. Kateb was the more rational opponent. He moved with a grace that was almost a dance. She quickly realized his goal was to tire Fuad, rather than hurt him.

"He can grant Fuad his life, can't he?" she asked Yusra.

"If the boy begs for mercy." She sounded doubtful. "Fuad is determined."

"He's not hurt yet. Kateb will wound him. I'm sure of it. He doesn't want Fuad dead."

"How can you know that?"

"I just know."

The fight continued. While Victoria didn't enjoy watching Kateb being attacked by a broadsword, she knew that he was by far the better fighter. Fuad didn't have a chance. She was even able to appreciate the sleeveless karate-type shirt he wore that left his impressive arms bare. Later, she would have to ask him to model it for her. Then she would take it off and…

No. That wasn't going to happen. She was leaving after the challenge. She couldn't stay. While his proposal had been tempting, she wouldn't trap herself in a half life where she almost had her heart's desire. In the short term, it would be fine, but eventually her heart would wither and die. There were—

Fuad dropped his broadsword. The crowd was instantly on its feet. Yusra crowed with delight, but Victoria knew something was terribly wrong. She felt it in her gut and cried out to Kateb to be careful.

Not that he could hear her over the thousands of screaming voices.

Being honorable, he lowered his sword to give Fuad time to retrieve his weapon. The teen bent down but instead of picking up the broadsword, he pulled a knife from his boot and stabbed it into Kateb's leg.

"Is that allowed?" she screamed.

"No, but not to worry. It's a small cut. Of no consequence. It will barely bleed."

"That's not the point," Victoria told her, not sure how she knew, but so very sure. A voice in her head screamed this is bad. Fuad had planned the moment. "It's not the cut, it's what's on the blade."

Even as she lunged for the half door that would open onto the field, Kateb dropped his sword and fell to his knees. Fuad grabbed his sword and lifted it above his head, obviously prepared to end his opponent's life.

"No!" she yelled as she ran. "No! You can't. You can't. I am the sacrifice."

Fuad stared at her. He was wild-eyed, his face pale. "Go away, woman. You have no place here."

Victoria heard other people running behind her. She nearly tripped on her stupid heels, but caught herself and raced up to thrust herself between Fuad and Kateb.

"I'm the sacrifice," she yelled in his face. "Me. You have to kill me. It's the law." She turned and saw several men bent over Kateb. "It's poison," she told them, frantic that he be saved in time. "I believe there's something on the knife blade."

Zayd hurried toward them, breathing heavily. He bent down and grabbed the knife, then sniffed the blade. Then he looked at Fuad.

"False revenge is meaningless, boy."

"Dead is dead," Fuad said angrily.

Victoria slapped him across the face. "What is wrong with you?" she demanded. "Your father's shame continues in you."

Fuad looked stunned and pointed the sword at her chest. "You want to die in his place, I will kill you."

"Fine," she yelled at him. "Do it, if you can. Kill me. Run me through. And then what? Your father is still dead.

Killed by a boy he kidnapped. A boy much younger than you, Fuad. Did you ever think about that? Kateb was just a kid. Do you think he wanted to hurt your father? He didn't have a choice—you do. At least you had the chance of a fair fight. That's more than your father gave Kateb. It's more than *you* gave him, too."

"Shut up," Fuad told her. "Stop talking at once."

"So you can kill me? Big Fuad kills a girl. That will make you proud."

There was activity going on behind her, but she didn't dare look. She could only hope they could save Kateb.

Fuad jabbed her arm with the sword. The point broke the skin and forced her back a few feet. Blood trickled down her arm and the wound hurt way more than she would have thought.

"You want to fight me," he jeered. "Fight me, sacrifice. If you are so eager to die, you will see death this day."

The fear was as real as the hatred burning in his eyes. Victoria didn't want to do this. She didn't want this to be her last day, her last breath. But there wasn't any choice.

"Pick up the sword," Fuad told her.

"You've got to be kidding. Do you know how much that weighs? I'm not picking it up. And even if I did, we both know I haven't got a clue what to do with it."

She sucked in a breath. "Okay, Fuad. Just do it. I'm going to stand here. I don't know what works best. Through the heart, I guess. But don't screw up. I'm not big on suffering. I'm a screamer and that's not how I want to go. So get it right the first time."

He blinked at her. "I will not kill an unarmed woman."

"Why not? You poisoned Kateb. What's the difference?"

He lowered his sword. "Why are you doing this? This is man's work."

"Dying? It think death is a universal experience. Everyone dies."

He glared at her. "Why are *you* doing this?" he asked again. "Why are *you* the sacrifice?"

"Because I love him too much to watch him die. He's my world. He's the only man I've ever loved." She fought to hold back tears. "Do you like torturing me? Is this fun for you?"

"I can't kill a woman."

"Why not? You were happy to do it a second ago." She stepped toward him. "I'm sorry about your dad. I lost my mom and it was really hard. My dad is a total loser. He gambles and he was never there when I was growing up. But my mom loved him and I never understood why—until now. Kateb isn't perfect, but he's a good man. He tries to do what's right. He'll lead the people into greatness. I believe that. But I'm still sorry about your dad."

Fuad started to shake. The sword slipped from his hands and fell to the dirt.

"No one has ever said that," he whispered, and began to cry. Victoria went to him and put her arms around him.

His sobs cut through her. For all his height and strength, he was still that small boy who had lost his father so many years ago.

"How do we end this?" she asked, still hugging him tight.

He raised his tear-streaked face and looked into her eyes. "Mercy," he whispered.

The guard led Fuad away. Victoria ran back to the elders' chambers and found Kateb lying on a makeshift bed. He was pale, but breathing.

"What happened?" she demanded, pushing her way to him. She dropped on her knees next to a man with a stethoscope around his neck. "Is he all right?"

"He will recover," the doctor told her. "The poison is

ancient and powerful, but easily reversed. In a few hours, Kateb will be back to normal."

"Thank God," she breathed, bent down and kissed him.

He opened his eyes.

"You make me insane," she said, not caring about the people around him. "I swear, I'd kill you myself if I thought it would make a difference. You nearly gave me a heart attack."

He smiled weakly. "You would kill me to teach me a lesson?"

"You know what I mean. Don't do that again."

"I will not." His gaze narrowed. "Why is there blood on your arm?"

"It's nothing."

He frowned. "I don't remember everything that happened, but I heard something about a sacrifice. Was that you?" He managed to sit up and look fairly intimidating, despite his weakened condition. "Is that true?" he demanded. "Were you the sacrifice?"

"Technically," she began.

He cut her off with a roar. "Who allowed this? Who accepted a woman as a sacrifice?"

"Hey," she said, poking him in the chest. "There's nothing that says a woman can't be the sacrifice. I looked it up."

"You don't read the ancient language."

"I had help. So what? You're not dead, I'm not dead. Fuad wants mercy. It's a good day."

"He needs to rest," the doctor said. "He must sleep for a few hours."

Victoria found herself being pulled away. She wanted to go with Kateb, but suddenly wasn't sure of her place. She'd told him she was leaving after the ceremony. He was fine, so shouldn't she go?

But leaving didn't seem so easy, all of a sudden. Life

without Kateb was impossible to imagine. She wanted more. She wanted a miracle.

Yusra led her into a side room. "That stupid boy," she murmured as she closed the door, then collected a bowl of water and began washing Victoria's still-stinging wound.

"What? He's fine. Mercy's allowed. You told me that."

"He tried to poison Kateb. Mercy only helps with the challenge. Attempted murder is a serious crime."

Victoria's stomach clenched. "Are you kidding? I know what he did was wrong, but there are reasons. His father dying. He was abandoned for years. It's surprising he managed to survive this long. So he's going to punished for all that?"

"The law requires it. Wouldn't your law insist he be punished?"

"Yes, but it's not completely his fault." So much for this being a good day. "What happens to him now?"

"There is a hearing. Today. Before sundown."

Victoria no longer felt the sting on her arm. "That fast?"

"Yes. There are thousands of witnesses. He will be convicted and sentenced."

She didn't want to know. "To what?"

"Death by the same poison he gave to Kateb. Fuad will die before sundown."

Still feeling the effects of the poison, Kateb made his way to the main hall in the palace. His doctor had given him something to sleep so his body could heal, and while Kateb appreciated the effort, he hadn't wanted to lose the day. There was too much to be done.

He knew the law, knew what would happen to Fuad. This was more pointless than the challenge, he thought grimly. An angry young man put to death. What would that solve? Any chance at reprieve was gone. He knew—he had sent for Victoria the moment he awoke and had been told she could not be found.

She had left, as she had told him she would. And he'd been the fool who let her go.

Zayd and the other elders walked into the hall ahead of him. They would proclaim him leader, then step aside so his first act would be to put Fuad to his death. Not a legacy that pleased Kateb.

Kateb walked to Zayd and knelt before him. The words were spoken and the crown of leadership placed on his head. At that moment he ceased to be what he had been before. He rose to the cheers of his people.

This was his destiny. He knew that—knew he was where he belonged. But nothing about this day was what he had expected. He had let Victoria go because he hadn't been willing to accept his own weakness. It wasn't that he didn't trust her—he didn't trust himself to survive her loss. He had loved Cantara and always would, but Victoria had touched him in a way no one ever had. She could see into his soul. She knew his flaws, his darkness and still she loved him. He was a better man for knowing her.

He must save Fuad. He saw that now. If he saved the boy, he would be worthy of the woman. But how? There was only one way and who would speak for a stranger who tried to commit murder?

Kateb walked to throne and called for Fuad to be brought to him.

The teenager was led in by guards. He was no longer defiant. Instead he appeared very young and very afraid.

Kateb waited until the room went quiet, then spoke. He read the charges and offered the petition signed by those who had witnessed the crime. Then he read the punishment—death by the same poison, to be administered before sundown.

Fuad bowed his head and sobbed.

"Is there one who will speak for the boy?" Kateb asked, scanning the crowd.

Only one was required. Someone who wasn't a member of Fuad's family or Kateb's. A single person to stand up to the accusers and say the boy was worth saving.

No one could be asked to speak for another. The responsibility lasted a lifetime. Should Fuad commit the same kind of crime ever again, the speaker would bear some of the blame.

Silence filled the large room. Defeat weighed on Kateb. Were he allowed to speak for Fuad, he would. But the law was clear. There had to be—

"I will speak for him," a voice called.

Kateb leaned forward as Victoria made her way to the front of the room.

She hadn't left. Relief lightened his heart and made him want to go to her. She was still here and someone had told her how to save Fuad.

She stepped next to Fuad and shooed away the guard. Then she took the boy's hand in hers and stared into his eyes.

"Tell me the truth," she said. "Do you want to die?"

He shook his head. "No. I thought… You're right. Revenge won't bring my father back. I'm sorry, too."

"Okay." She turned to Kateb. "I speak for him."

"You were the sacrifice," he said, knowing that he would never be worthy of her but more than willing to spend the rest of his life trying. And later he would talk to the elders about letting Victoria nearly give up her life for his.

"I've never been one before. You know how I love getting in the middle of things."

He did his best not to smile. There were formalities to be worked through. "Do you know Fuad?"

"Not well."

"Do you understand the responsibility of what you do?"

"And people say *I* talk too much." She nodded. "Yes. For the rest of his life, what he does reflects on me. If he screws up, he is so going to pay." She glanced at the boy. "You know that, right?"

"Yes. But I won't."

"I've heard that before." She turned back to Kateb. "I have a plan. I called the Bahanian palace and spoke to one of the princes there. Fuad will be given a job in the stable. I've heard he's good with horses. They'll watch him and take care of him. He'll get a fresh start. Maybe go to night school. There's a retired policeman who will give him a place to stay."

"Why do you do this?" Kateb asked.

She frowned. "Yusra didn't say that was one of the questions."

"*I* am asking. Why would you bother? You said you don't know Fuad. What is this to you?"

She drew in a breath. "I feel bad for him. He lost his father when he was young and he was basically abandoned. You're going to work on changing that, right? See what happens when a society doesn't take care of its children?"

He held in a smile. "Yes. I will do something about it."

"Good. I don't think Fuad is bad. I think he's angry. There's a difference. I want to give him a chance."

"Is that the only reason?"

"No. I knew you didn't want him to die. I'm doing this for you."

Around them, people started whispering. He ignored them, ignored everything but the woman before him. The woman he loved.

He wasn't sure why he hadn't seen it before. Maybe all

the steps were required before he could get to this point. Like Fuad, he'd been given a second chance.

"If I grant Fuad his life," he said. "What will you give me in return?"

Victoria put her hands on her hips. "Excuse me? Haven't I done enough today? I put my life on the line for you, mister. I was willing to die for you. I think the real question is what are you going to do for me?"

"We will deal with Fuad first," he said, and looked at the teenager. "Do you accept Victoria's arrangements?"

Fuad nodded. "Yes. I yield to her wisdom, even though she is a woman."

Victoria rolled her eyes.

"You will go to Bahania in the morning," Kateb told him. "I will come see you in a month and we will talk about how you are doing. You are given a second chance, Fuad. Use it well."

The guards led him away.

"Now that we're done with that," Victoria said. "You didn't answer my question."

He smiled. "I am the leader of the desert people and you are a mere woman. It is up to you to give to me."

"If you think I won't embarrass you in front of this crowd, you are seriously wrong." But she wasn't angry. He could see the humor brightening her eyes. Humor and something else that gave him hope....

"This is what I want," he said, ignoring her threat. "I want all the days you have left. I want your heart, your soul, your body, as my own. I want your children, your future, your wisdom, your laughter. I want all of you, Victoria McCallan."

She drew in a breath. "That's a lot," she whispered. "Why should I agree?"

"You will make me say it in public?"

"If you can't say it in front of your people, what does it matter?"

He rose and walked toward her. He cupped her face in his hands and stared into her eyes. "I love you. I have loved you from the first moment I saw you, but I fought it. I told myself you were not worthy. Then I told myself you were not to be trusted. Then I told myself you were trying to trick me."

"You need to stop talking to yourself so much," she said with a smile.

"Apparently." He brushed his hand along her cheek. "I offer you all that I have, all that I am. I will love you with my last breath. You outshine the sun. You are my world. Stay with me, marry me. Love me."

She put her hands on his chest. "Okay."

"That's it? Usually you have more to say."

"Not today."

"You love me?"

"I've said it like forty times."

"I want to hear it again."

"You are so demanding." She laughed. "I love you, Kateb." Everyone began to cheer.

"You'll marry me?" he asked over the noise.

"Yes."

"Good." He bent down and kissed her. "You know this means you're going to be a princess. You'll be able to buy all the shoes you want."

"That's a lot of shoes," she said with a laugh.

He smiled. "It's a big palace."

Epilogue

Victoria lay on the pillows in front of the Christmas tree. To her right, a fire burned brightly, which would have been a little warm, but the ceiling fan helped stir the air. Kateb stretched out next to her, his arm around her.

"Did you have a good day?" she asked.

"It was a Christmas like no other."

"I probably went a little overboard," she admitted, thinking that bringing in forty trees for the palace could be considered excessive, but she'd never had an unlimited budget before.

"Everything was beautiful. The twinkle lights were a big hit. Last night was especially popular."

She rolled toward him and propped her chin on his chest. "I thought the kids would like being read 'The Night

Before Christmas.' My mom used to read it to me when I was young."

Her handsome husband smiled at her. "I'm sorry I didn't have the chance to meet her."

"Me, too. She would have been impressed."

"Are you impressed?"

She laughed. "Most days."

"Good."

She stood and stretched, then walked to the large tree. In the back, tucked between two big branches, was one last present. She grabbed the small box and carried it back to Kateb.

"For you," she said, sitting cross-legged in front of him.

He sat up and frowned. "I have nothing more for you."

"You gave me plenty. Five pairs of shoes, diamonds, clothes shopping in Paris... The only thing missing really was a pony."

"Did you want a pony?"

"No. I want to give you this."

"But I am content with all I have, my love. You were most generous."

"You'll want this. Trust me."

She handed him the box. Before he opened it, he leaned in and kissed her, then pulled off the ribbon.

She hadn't been sure until just a few days ago. The timing had made her crazy and she'd needed Yusra's help to get the present. It wasn't like she could just go buy it in the marketplace. Not if she wanted to keep it a secret.

Now she watched as the man she loved, who made it clear every day just how much he loved her, lifted the cover off the small box and pulled out a tiny pair of yellow baby booties. His gaze dropped to her stomach, then returned to her eyes.

"Are you sure?"

"I've peed on a stick and everything. Which wasn't easy. There's nowhere for your wife to buy a pregnancy test in the village. Or buy booties. I had to send for both of them. It's been nerve-racking. But I wanted to be sure." She bit her lower lip. "Are you happy? I want you to be happy."

He pulled her into his arms and kissed her. "Thank you," he whispered. "Thank you."

His dark eyes gleamed with pride and pleasure. His arms were, as always, a safe haven. He'd given her the world…and his heart. She couldn't ask for more.

* * * * *

*Want more Susan Mallery? Look out for
HIGH-POWERED, HOT-BLOODED,
available in December from Silhouette Desire.*

Duncan Patrick may have been named the country's meanest CEO, but he might have met his match in the most unlikely of women. Kindergarten teacher Annie McCoy is going toe-to-toe with Duncan, if only to save her brother, who has been caught embezzling from Duncan's company. Despite her innocent looks, Annie is tough and determined to keep her brother out of jail. But Duncan is as handsome and charismatic as her and is ruthless when he wants to be. And he wants Annie as his mistress…. Will Annie fall for his charms, or will Duncan be the one who falls first?

*Celebrate 60 years of pure reading pleasure
with Harlequin®!*

To commemorate the event, Silhouette Special Edition invites you to Ashley O'Ballivan's bed-and-breakfast in the small town of Stone Creek. The beautiful innkeeper will have her hands full caring for her old flame Jack McCall. He's on the run and recovering from a mysterious illness, but that won't stop him from trying to win Ashley back.

*Enjoy an exclusive glimpse of Linda Lael Miller's
AT HOME IN STONE CREEK
Available in November 2009
from Silhouette Special Edition®.*

The helicopter swung abruptly sideways in a dizzying arch, setting Jack McCall's fever-ravaged brain spinning.

His friend's voice sounded tinny, coming through the earphones. "You belong in a hospital," he said. "Not some backwater bed-and-breakfast."

All Jack really knew about the virus raging through his system was that it wasn't contagious, and there was no known treatment for it besides a lot of rest and quiet. "I don't like hospitals," he responded, hoping he sounded like his normal self. "They're full of sick people."

Vince Griffin chuckled but it was a dry sound, rough at the edges. "What's in Stone Creek, Arizona?" he asked. "Besides a whole lot of nothin'?"

Ashley O'Ballivan was in Stone Creek, and she was a whole lot of somethin', but Jack had neither the strength nor the inclination to explain. After the way he'd ducked out six months before, he didn't expect a welcome, knew he didn't deserve one. But Ashley, being Ashley, would take him in whatever her misgivings.

He had to get to Ashley; he'd be all right.

He closed his eyes, letting the fever swallow him.

There was no telling how much time had passed when he became aware of the chopper blades slowing overhead. Dimly, he saw the private ambulance waiting on the airfield outside of Stone Creek; it seemed that twilight had descended.

Jack sighed with relief. His clothes felt clammy against his flesh. His teeth began to chatter as two figures unloaded a gurney from the back of the ambulance and waited for the blades to stop.

"Great," Vince remarked, unsnapping his seat belt. "Those two look like volunteers, not real EMTs."

The chopper bounced sickeningly on its runners, and Vince, with a shake of his head, pushed open his door and jumped to the ground, head down.

Jack waited, wondering if he'd be able to stand on his own. After fumbling unsuccessfully with the buckle on his seat belt, he decided not.

When it was safe the EMTs approached, following Vince, who opened Jack's door.

His old friend Tanner Quinn stepped around Vince, his grin not quite reaching his eyes.

"You look like hell warmed over," he told Jack cheerfully.

"Since when are you an EMT?" Jack retorted.

Tanner reached in, wedged a shoulder under Jack's right arm and hauled him out of the chopper. His knees immediately buckled, and Vince stepped up, supporting him on the other side.

"In a place like Stone Creek," Tanner replied, "everybody helps out."

They reached the wheeled gurney, and Jack found himself on his back.

Tanner and the second man strapped him down, a process that brought back a few bad memories.

"Is there even a hospital in this place?" Vince asked irritably from somewhere in the night.

"There's a pretty good clinic over in Indian Rock," Tanner answered easily, "and it isn't far to Flagstaff." He paused to help his buddy hoist Jack and the gurney into the back of the ambulance. "You're in good hands, Jack. My wife is the best veterinarian in the state."

Jack laughed raggedly at that.

Vince muttered a curse.

Tanner climbed into the back beside him, perched on some kind of fold-down seat. The other man shut the doors.

"You in any pain?" Tanner said as his partner climbed into the driver's seat and started the engine.

"No." Jack looked up at his oldest and closest friend and wished he'd listened to Vince. Ever since he'd come down with the virus—a week after snatching a five-year-old girl back from her non-custodial parent, a small-time Colombian drug dealer—he hadn't been able to think about anyone or anything but Ashley. When he *could* think, anyway.

Now, in one of the first clearheaded moments he'd experienced since checking himself out of Bethesda the day before, he realized he might be making a major mistake. Not by facing Ashley—he owed her that much and a lot more. No, he could be putting her in danger, putting Tanner and his daughter and his pregnant wife in danger, too.

"I shouldn't have come here," he said, keeping his voice low.

Tanner shook his head, his jaw clamped down hard as though he was irritated by Jack's statement.

"This is where you belong," Tanner insisted. "If you'd

had sense enough to know that six months ago, old buddy, when you bailed on Ashley without so much as a fare-thee-well, you wouldn't be in this mess."

Ashley. The name had run through his mind a million times in those six months, but hearing somebody say it out loud was like having a fist close around his insides and squeeze hard.

Jack couldn't speak.

Tanner didn't press for further conversation.

The ambulance bumped over country roads, finally hitting smooth blacktop.

"Here we are," Tanner said. "Ashley's place."

* * * * *

Will Jack be able to patch things up with Ashley,
or will his past put the woman he loves in harm's way?
Find out in
AT HOME IN STONE CREEK
by Linda Lael Miller
Available November 2009
from Silhouette Special Edition®.

**This November,
Silhouette Special Edition®
brings you**

NEW YORK TIMES
BESTSELLING AUTHOR

LINDA LAEL
MILLER

At Home in
Stone Creek

*Available in November
wherever books are sold.*

Silhouette Desire

**FROM *NEW YORK TIMES*
BESTSELLING AUTHOR**

DIANA
PALMER

THE
MAVERICK

**A BRAND-NEW
LONG, TALL
TEXAN STORY**

Visit Silhouette Books at www.eHarlequin.com

SD76982

HARLEQUIN *Romance*.

This November,
queen of the rugged rancher

PATRICIA THAYER

teams up with

DONNA ALWARD

*to bring you an extra-special treat
this holiday season—*
two romantic stories
in one book!

Join sisters Amelia and Kelley for Christmas at
Rocking H Ranch where these feisty cowgirls swap
presents for proposals, mistletoe for marriage and
experience the unbeatable rush of falling in love!

Available in November wherever books are sold.

HR17619

HARLEQUIN
Ambassadors

Want to share your passion for reading Harlequin® Books?

Become a Harlequin Ambassador!

Harlequin Ambassadors are a group of passionate and well-connected readers who are willing to share their joy of reading Harlequin® books with family and friends.

You'll be sent all the tools you need to spark great conversation, including free books!

All we ask is that you share the romance with your friends and family!

You'll also be invited to have a say in new book ideas and exchange opinions with women just like you!

To see if you qualify* to be a Harlequin Ambassador, please visit www.HarlequinAmbassadors.com.

*Please note that not everyone who applies to be a Harlequin Ambassador will qualify. For more information please visit www.HarlequinAmbassadors.com.

Thank you for your participation.

REQUEST YOUR FREE BOOKS!
2 FREE NOVELS PLUS 2 FREE GIFTS!

SPECIAL EDITION®
Life, Love and Family!

YES! Please send me 2 FREE Silhouette Special Edition® novels and my 2 FREE gifts (gifts are worth about $10). After receiving them, if I don't wish to receive any more books, I can return the shipping statement marked "cancel." If I don't cancel, I will receive 6 brand-new novels every month and be billed just $4.24 per book in the U.S. or $4.99 per book in Canada. That's a savings of at least 15% off the cover price! It's quite a bargain! Shipping and handling is just 50¢ per book.* I understand that accepting the 2 free books and gifts places me under no obligation to buy anything. I can always return a shipment and cancel at any time. Even if I never buy another book from Silhouette, the two free books and gifts are mine to keep forever.

235 SDN EYN4 335 SDN EYPG

Name	(PLEASE PRINT)	
Address		Apt. #
City	State/Prov.	Zip/Postal Code

Signature (if under 18, a parent or guardian must sign)

Mail to the Silhouette Reader Service:
IN U.S.A.: P.O. Box 1867, Buffalo, NY 14240-1867
IN CANADA: P.O. Box 609, Fort Erie, Ontario L2A 5X3

Not valid to current subscribers of Silhouette Special Edition books.

Want to try two free books from another line?
Call 1-800-873-8635 or visit www.morefreebooks.com.

* Terms and prices subject to change without notice. Prices do not include applicable taxes. Sales tax applicable in N.Y. Canadian residents will be charged applicable provincial taxes and GST. Offer not valid in Quebec. This offer is limited to one order per household. All orders subject to approval. Credit or debit balances in a customer's account(s) may be offset by any other outstanding balance owed by or to the customer. Please allow 4 to 6 weeks for delivery. Offer available while quantities last.

Your Privacy: Silhouette is committed to protecting your privacy. Our Privacy Policy is available online at www.eHarlequin.com or upon request from the Reader Service. From time to time we make our lists of customers available to reputable third parties who may have a product or service of interest to you. If you would prefer we not share your name and address, please check here. ☐

SSE09R

Silhouette®

COMING NEXT MONTH

Available October 27, 2009

#2005 AT HOME IN STONE CREEK—Linda Lael Miller
Sometimes Ashley O'Ballivan felt like the only single woman left in Stone Creek. All because of security expert Jack McCall—the man who broke her heart years ago. Now Jack was mysteriously back in town…and Ashley's single days were numbered.

#2006 A LAWMAN FOR CHRISTMAS—Marie Ferrarella
Kate's Boys
When a car accident landed her mother in the hospital, it was Kelsey Marlowe's worst nightmare. Luckily, policeman Morgan Donnelly was there to save her mom, and the nightmare turned into a dream come true—as Kelsey fell hard for the sexy lawman!

#2007 QUINN McCLOUD'S CHRISTMAS BRIDE—Lois Faye Dyer
The McClouds of Montana
Wolf Creek's temporary sheriff Quinn McCloud was a wanderer; librarian Abigail Foster was the type to set down roots. But when they joined forces to help a little girl left on Abigail's doorstep, did opposites ever attract! And just in time for a Christmas wedding.

#2008 THE TEXAN'S DIAMOND BRIDE—Teresa Hill
The Foleys and the McCords
When Travis Foley caught gemologist Paige McCord snooping around on his property for the fabled Santa Magdalena Diamond, it spelled trouble for the feuding families. But what was it about this irresistible interloper that gave the rugged rancher pause?

#2009 MERRY CHRISTMAS, COWBOY!—Cindy Kirk
Meet Me in Montana
All academic Lauren Van Meveren wanted from her trip to Big Sky country was peace and quiet to write her dissertation. But when she moved onto widower Seth Anderssen's ranch to help with his daughter, Lauren got the greatest gift of all—true love.

#2010 MOONLIGHT AND MISTLETOE—Dawn Temple
When her estranged father sent Beverly Hills attorney Kyle Anderson to strong-arm her into a settlement, Shayna Miller was determined to resist…until Kyle melted her heart and had her heading for the nearest mistletoe, head-over-heels in love….

SSECNMBPA1009